Praise for the Kate Kennedy Mysteries

"A charming new series that sparkles like the south Florida sunshine . . . Kate Kennedy is a warm and funny heroine . . . An ideal beach read . . . Sure to please."
— Nancy Martin, author of the Blackbird Sisters Mysteries

"Miss Marple with a modern twist."
— Donna Andrews, Agatha and Anthony Award–winning author of *You've Got Murder* and *Delete All Suspects*

"Kate Kennedy will make you laugh and keep you on the edge of your seat until the very last page."
— Victoria Thompson, author of the Gaslight Mysteries

"The characters in this new series are terrific. Nora Charles has done a great job creating the characters and setting for the story. I look forward to reading many more in the series and highly recommend this book." — *Mystery Morgue*

"Excellent . . . [an] entertaining read."
— *The Romance Reader's Connection*

"*Death Is a Bargain* is another top-notch entry in a great series." — Carolyn Hart, author of *Death of the Party*

"A fun take on an English village cozy with an endearing heroine, *Death with an Ocean View* is a quick read that has potential to become a favorite with young and old alike."
— *The Mystery Reader*

W9-CFK-018

Hurricane Homicide

NORA CHARLES

BERKLEY PRIME CRIME, NEW YORK

THE BERKLEY PUBLISHING GROUP
Published by the Penguin Group
Penguin Group (USA) Inc.
375 Hudson Street, New York, New York 10014, USA
Penguin Group (Canada), 90 Eglinton Avenue East, Suite 700, Toronto, Ontario M4P 2Y3, Canada
(a division of Pearson Penguin Canada Inc.)
Penguin Books Ltd., 80 Strand, London WC2R 0RL, England
Penguin Group Ireland, 25 St. Stephen's Green, Dublin 2, Ireland (a division of Penguin Books Ltd.)
Penguin Group (Australia), 250 Camberwell Road, Camberwell, Victoria 3124, Australia
(a division of Pearson Australia Group Pty. Ltd.)
Penguin Books India Pvt. Ltd., 11 Community Centre, Panchsheel Park, New Delhi—110 017, India
Penguin Group (NZ), Cnr. Airborne and Rosedale Roads, Albany, Auckland 1310, New Zealand
(a division of Pearson New Zealand Ltd.)
Penguin Books (South Africa) (Pty.) Ltd., 24 Sturdee Avenue, Rosebank, Johannesburg 2196,
South Africa

Penguin Books Ltd., Registered Offices: 80 Strand, London WC2R 0RL, England

This is a work of fiction. Names, characters, places, and incidents either are the product of the author's imagination or are used fictitiously, and any resemblance to actual persons, living or dead, business establishments, events, or locales is entirely coincidental. The publisher does not have any control over and does not assume any responsibility for author or third-party websites or their content.

HURRICANE HOMICIDE

A Berkley Prime Crime Book / published by arrangement with the author

PRINTING HISTORY
Berkley Prime Crime mass-market edition / December 2006

Copyright © 2006 by Norren Wald.
Cover art by Hiro Kimura.
Cover design by Rita Frangie.

ISBN: 0-425-21312-9

BERKLEY® PRIME CRIME
Berkley Prime Crime Books are published by The Berkley Publishing Group,
a division of Penguin Group (USA) Inc.,
375 Hudson Street, New York, New York 10014.
The name BERKLEY PRIME CRIME and the BERKLEY PRIME CRIME design are trademarks
belonging to Penguin Group (USA) Inc.

PRINTED IN THE UNITED STATES OF AMERICA

10 9 8 7 6 5 4 3 2 1

To Steve with love

Acknowledgments

My gratitude to my friends, colleagues, and loved ones—some fall into all three categories—who have helped shape, edit, and/or promote my novels: Donna Andrews, Nancy Beardsley, Cordelia Benedict, Helen Brennan, Carla Coupe, Ellen Crosby, Diane and Dave Dufour, Laura Durham, Peggy Hanson, Doris Holland, Barbara Giorgio, Susan Kavanagh, Valerie Patterson, Gail Prensky, Billy Reckdenwald, Pat Sanders, Dr. Diane Shirer, Steve Smith, Gloria and Paul Stuart, Joyce Sweeney, and Sandi Wilson. And, thanks to my editor, Tom Colgan, and my agent, Peter Rubie. They're the best.

one

"Don't ya just wanna kill him?" Rosie O'Grady, a retired Radio City Rockette, asked Kate Kennedy. "Such a phony-baloney." Rosie's raspy Bronx accent came across loud and clear.

Kate's Westie, Ballou, ran back and forth along the shoreline, scattering sand on Rosie's pedicure. He'd been yapping and agitated since Kate and Rosie had set up their beach chairs. The little dog was trying to tell her something. But what?

A few feet away, the object of Rosie's murderous wrath, Uncle Weatherwise, South Florida's answer to Willard Scott and Al Roker, and Ocean Vista's newest resident, held court at the water's edge.

Rosie's question, though amplified by the sea breeze, fell on Weatherwise's partially deaf ears. The fat man smiled and nodded in response to his fawning fans' patter as white-capped waves crashed against his feet. Kate doubted he could hear a word anyone said.

"Trust me, Kate, he's no good. " Unlike her neighbors, longtime admirers of the seventy-something local television icon, Ocean Vista's Program Chair Rosie, eighty-four and still kicking, had cast the lone dissenting vote when the condo board approved Walt Weatherwise's owner/member application.

Nodding, Kate tried to appear neutral, though she'd disliked Weatherwise at first sight, sensing something strange, yet eerily familiar, about the smiling, rotund weatherman.

Rosie wiped away sweat beads dancing across her upper lip. Late August in Palmetto Beach—even with the setting sun, their beach chairs planted in damp sand, and their feet washed with an occasional wave—was like being burned at the stake . . . by choice. Kate missed Jones Beach where summer's twilight held a hint of autumn.

"Weatherwise's teddy bear TV image is a cover. He's full of it and full of himself. For starters, he's not from the Midwest. Back when I was a hoofer, he used to pal around with the mob in Manhattan."

"The mob?" Kate asked, surprised. "Really?"

Rosie arched her right foot, disturbing Ballou's relentless pacing. Whining, he made a sharp turn, walking over his mistress's toes, in dire need of a pedicure. "Weatherwise is a wiseguy. I know, Kate. I dated Albert Anastasia, before he got bumped off in the old Park Sheraton's barbershop."

Kate smiled, remembering that a lifetime ago her father, who'd worked two blocks away on Fifth Avenue, had his hair cut at the hotel, too.

A gust of warm wind blew Kate's favorite Southampton straw hat into the water. An agile Rosie scrambled out of her beach chair to rescue it.

"Thanks." Kate smiled at the lithe octogenarian and plopped her hat back onto her head. Maybe her yoga exercises weren't enough. Maybe she should enroll in Rosie's dance class.

Lucy Diamond, the condo's bylaws chair, sauntered over to Weatherwise's circle. The tall brunette was not one of his fans. "Just call me Uncle" had blown into his first condo board meeting and brewed up a tempest in a coffeepot, demanding that Lucy's committee amend the bylaws so that he could plant medicinal marijuana on his terrace. Lucy, a retired federal prosecutor, hadn't been amused.

"He's a lousy weatherman, too." Rosie raised her voice, shaking a head full of steel-gray curls. "We shoulda canceled this year's clambake. These old bones tell me we're in for a storm. *Today.*" She stamped her foot in the sand.

Ballou ran back from the ocean, dug his feet into the sand, and barked sharply at Kate. What was wrong with the Westie?

Could Uncle be off track with Hurricane Harriet? He'd predicted landfall in Key West. *Tonight.* The residents in the Keys had been evacuated.

Walt Weatherwise was renowned for tracking a hurricane's path, and his colorful forecasts leading up to a storm's hit or miss got higher ratings than the final episode of *M*A*S*H*.

Kate stood, too, irked that she couldn't get up and out of a beach chair with the dancer's grace. A darkening sky and turbulent sea made her wonder if Rosie was right. Did

Ballou smell danger? Should Palmetto Beach residents
have gone shopping for duct tape along with their neighbors to the south? And, instead of roasting corn and clams
in a brand-new garbage can—that Kate had shopped for
herself—should they be getting ready to evacuate?

The moonlighting lifeguard, hired for the evening's
festivities—as Marlene Friedman, Kate's former sister-in-
law, lifelong best friend, and condo president had explained—"Every year at least one old goat with a bellyful
of beer swims out too far and decides he's drowning"—
was on his cell phone, his left hand gesturing toward the
sea, his mouth moving, his words inaudible.

"Yo, Kate!" Marlene, wearing a scarlet polka-dot tank-
ini, a deep tan, and a frown, waved an ear of corn and
shouted over the garbage can. During a fleeting moment
of romantic interest in Uncle Weatherwise, Marlene had
volunteered to serve as sous chef at the clambake.
"Raindrops are falling on my . . ." The wind whipped
away the last of Marlene's lyrics and blew Kate's beach
chair into the ocean.

"My God, look, the water's up to my knees!" Lucy's
alarm proved contagious. The crowd around Uncle
Weatherwise moved like lemmings in reverse, away from
the sea.

The rains came—hard, driving, relentless. The navy
sky went black. A siren roared. Soaking wet, Kate
clutched Ballou's leash with one hand and reached for
Rosie with the other. The wind, now wicked, lashed across
Kate's face. She staggered, losing her balance in the wet
sand. Rosie grabbed Kate's arm, helped her up, then, with
Ballou glued to Kate's heels, they trudged toward Ocean
Vista, the wind at their backs pummeling them.

"Everyone off the beach!" The lifeguard shouted through a megaphone. "Now. Move it! Get off the beach!"

Napkins, plastic pitchers, plates, and small beach chairs were flying around with the squawking seagulls. A plastic knife struck and stuck in Lucy's forehead, drawing blood. Kate, wanting to scream herself, thought Lucy could be heard in Boca.

Marlene, overweight but toned, dropped her beach bag, and half-carried Lucy toward the condo.

Wiping sand from her eyes, Kate saw Uncle Weatherwise reach the pool first. His long legs made the fat man leader of his fans. Or, maybe, former fans: Weatherwise dashed straight toward the condo's back door, letting the pool gate swing shut. Skinny Bob Seeley, the condo's finance chair, a surprising second, held the gate open for those behind him. Marlene dragged Lucy through the door, then returned to relieve Bob.

Proud of Marlene, Kate reached down, lifted Ballou, and said, "Come on, Rosie, we're almost home." Then she whispered in the Westie's ear, "I should have listened to you, Ballou."

"Ain't I the one who got us here?" Rosie's rasp came out as close to a shout as decades of unfiltered Chesterfields allowed.

Kate, feeling guilty for taking the credit, laughed. A mistake. Sand coated her teeth like toothpaste.

Why hadn't she gone to Martha's Vineyard with Kevin and his family? Her daughter-in-law, Jennifer, had predicted, "August in Florida, Kate? You'll be sorry." A seer as well as a stockbroker?

Ocean Vista's residents, on what seemed like a daily basis, dismissed clouds by quoting the Palmetto Beach Chamber of Commerce's party line: "If you don't like the weather in South Florida, wait five minutes." And, often as not, to Kate's annoyance, the sun would appear. Even in her panic, she savored the reverse irony.

"The U.S. Weather Service," the lifeguard's voice broke as he yelled into his megaphone, "now reports that Palmetto Beach is in the direct path of Hurricane Harriet."

TWO

They had less than ninety minutes to evacuate.

Kate spent six of those minutes in the shower. No way would she leave full of sand. She washed, then finger-combed her short silver hair, and put on moisturizer and lipstick. How long would they be gone? She threw her cosmetic case in her toiletries bag and checked her watch. Seventy-five minutes left to transport all of Palmetto Beach's residents over to the mainland.

Policemen had been driving their patrol cars up and down A1A, sirens blaring, shouting instructions, asking residents to line up in front of their condos as soon as possible, stressing the Neptune Boulevard Bridge was backed up for miles, and the evacuees must carpool, six to a vehicle, and, most frightening, that the bridge would close at nine P.M.

She and Marlene were to meet in the lobby in ten minutes, then carpool with Rosie O'Grady, Lucy Diamond,

Bob Seeley, and Walt Weatherwise, in the latter's SUV. Not Kate's idea. Rosie's. And how bizarre was that?

Prioritizing, she tossed Ballou's dog food and her Pepcid AC into a large green cloth Barnes & Noble shopping bag and, stumped, wondered what else she should take. Tissues. Underwear. A sweatshirt. Money. ID.

Kate felt grateful to be living in Ocean Vista. Public high schools and other large hurricane shelters didn't accept pets. Most condos on the beach would be enforcing the strict evacuation rules that had been agreed upon, then signed and sealed at closing: Residents were required to leave their pets with family or friends on the mainland before proceeding to a shelter.

But Ocean Vista had a secret weapon: Bob Seeley, an elder at St. Thomas Episcopal Church in Coral Reef. And St. Thomas's pastor had offered its high-school gym as refuge for the Ocean Vista residents *and* their animals.

Coral Reef was fifteen miles west of 95. Should she bring a pillow?

Would she be coming back?

The misanthrope in the apartment next to hers didn't think so.

When Kate, holding Ballou, had been struggling to open her front door with a wet, sandy hand, her neighbor popped out into the hall, screaming that no one would ever make it, the island and everyone on it would be swept away, and Ocean Vista would crumble into the sand. Then, vowing to go down with the condo, she'd darted into her apartment.

What if Harriet left Kate with nothing? Images of Katrina's and Rita's destruction and their ravaged victims flooded her head. Could she, too, end up homeless? Could the wind hammering her windows become strong enough to destroy Ocean Vista?

Kate scurried, unexpected tears spilling down her cheeks, pulling photos of her grandaughters from the bookcase's bottom shelf, shoving them into the tote bag. She rushed to the bedroom, Ballou at her heels, grabbed Charlie's wedding ring from her top bureau drawer, then ran back to the living room.

She stopped short in front of the TV.

"The hospital evacuation is well under way, though the Neptune Boulevard Bridge is backed up for two miles to the south." Uncle Weatherwise's stand-in sounded deadly serious. "Chief Wilson has ordered all A1A residents to leave their homes immediately. The police expect to have everyone off island by nine P.M. The eye of Hurricane Harriet should hit around eleven. Please leave now." He seemed to be staring at Kate. "Do not delay."

Confirming the weatherman's warning, rain slammed against the sliding glass doors that led to her balcony. Kate watched water seep in, staining her wall-to-wall off-white carpet. She dashed to the linen closet, grabbed a pile of towels, and tried to stem the tide. Useless: her ocean view was now a liability rather than an asset.

She'd had Channel Eight on all through her evacuation preparation. The station's somewhat subdued hurricane-countdown watch—less of the usual hype and soap-opera style coverage that dragged on for days, and often ended in anticlimactic shortfalls or total misses—scared Kate more than the high drama.

Uncle's stand-in, a nerdy young man, dressed in a slicker, ready to evacuate himself, tried hard to reassure his audience. Throughout his reportage, his voice re-

mained calm and soft, but a slight tremor transmitted his
fear.

Ready to roll, Kate yanked her cell phone out of her
sweatpants' pocket and dialed her sister-in-law. Her fingers shook. She sank into a chair. Ballou licked her hand.

"We're out of here," Marlene said.

Kate held the Westie on a tight leash as they left the
apartment. Like Scarlett O'Hara locking the Yankees out
of Aunt Pittypat's house in Atlanta, she bolted the door behind her.

Charlie had dropped dead still clutching the pen he'd
used to close on the condo. Kate had so resented living
here alone. Ocean Vista had been Charlie's dream retire-
ment and, since they'd sold her beloved Tudor in
Rockville Centre, she didn't have anywhere to go. Over
the last year, she'd come to accept, even feel part of,
Palmetto Beach. Be careful what you wish for. Would
Kate retroactively get what she'd wanted? Or worse, what
she deserved?

Ballou and Kate rode the elevator alone. He nuzzled
her cheek. She allowed herself three sobs. One per floor.

Pandemonium reigned in the lobby. Well, with all the faux
marble, gilt-framed mirrors, and glass floor-to-ceiling
front doors, it appeared to have been decorated for just
such an occasion. Kate took perverse pleasure in her snide
thought.

Hoards of her neighbors, all clamoring at once, clus-
tered around the huge center fountain celebrating mixed
myths: An alabaster statue of the Greek Goddess
Aphrodite cavorting with the Roman Cupid. Dozens of
Roman Cupids.

Her friends' fear, matching her own, sobered Kate; she felt ashamed for being so damn judgmental.

"Kate." Marlene startled her. "Over here. Turn left at the first potted palm."

The thick crowd made it impossible to find any landmark. She headed toward the strained sound of her sister-in-law's voice.

Marlene wore a plum jogging suit with matching sneakers, her lipstick and eye shadow were color coordinated, too, and she'd styled her platinum hair in her trademark French twist. She carried a tote bag the size of a small trunk and her feet were surrounded by a matching set of Louis Vitton luggage.

"There will be five other people in the car, Marlene."

"So?"

"Whadda ya crazy?" Rosie O'Grady popped out from behind the fake plant. "Or just a selfish old broad? There ain't no room in Weatherwise's car for all those suitcases. Talk about dumb blondes."

A wide-eyed, but silent, Marlene stared at the older woman. Had she been rendered speechless?

Kate stifled a giggle.

"Please allow me to help carry the bags back to your condo, Marlene." Bob Seeley, ever polite, spoke with a sense of urgency. "As you know, I'm assisting in the evacuation effort and the police have just advised me that Walt Weatherwise is third in line to pick up his passengers at the front door."

Without a word, Marlene placed a smaller suitcase on top of a larger one, and pulled them toward the elevator. Bob grabbed the duffel bag and followed in her wake.

•   •   •

Kate, squeezed in the backseat between Marlene and Lucy—
the latter opting to sit as far away from Uncle Weatherwise as possible, had claimed the right rear passenger seat
as her own—squirmed, but couldn't get comfortable. A
Mercedes SUV with a front bench seat should provide
more room for their fat-cat customers.

In the front, the tall but slim Rosie sat in the middle,
the too thin Bob Seeley to her right. With Uncle's girth
spilling over into Rosie's turf, Kate had no complaints.

Conversation turned out to be as constricted as the passengers: Weatherwise babbling about the storm and its
poor coverage with him out of the loop; Rosie and
Marlene jabbing at each other; Bob and Kate acting as
peacemakers; and Lucy's silence getting on everyone's
nerves.

And, after more than an hour in the car, its windshield
pelted by rain and the ever-increasing wind whistling
through its windows, they weren't going anywhere.

"We still haven't turned onto Neptune Boulevard."
Rosie had stated the obvious.

Marlene groaned, but a sharp rap on the driver's side
stifled her retort.

Uncle Weatherwise opened the rear window. Kate
started as rain soaked the SUV's backseat.

"Everyone out of the car," a cop shouted. "Hurry up,
folks. We're forming a human chain and walking across."

The nine P.M. bridge closing deadline was less than ten
minutes away.

Three

A soaked Kate, linked hand to hand between a young policeman—who had Ballou tucked under his left arm—and Marlene, stumbled, bringing the human chain to an abrupt halt.

"Don't look down," she told herself, startled to hear her own voice, not realizing she'd spoken aloud. Tonight, the Intercoastal Waterway far below the bridge seemed as rough and forbidding as the North Atlantic.

The moon's intermittent appearances between the dark clouds, together with the cops' flashlights, provided spotty light.

God knows the rain-dimmed headlights of the cars jamming both the incoming and outgoing lanes as they inched west toward the mainland were of no help.

"You bastard!" Someone shouted. Could that be Rosie's rasp?

Kate spun around, again losing her balance as the wind

slapped her face. She broke her fall, and wobbly, let go of
Marlene's hand to grab the railing on the bridge's narrow,
slippery footpath. Uncle Weatherwise, several links behind, dropped someone's hand to raise his arm in a threatening gesture aimed at the person behind him. A tall, slim
figure. Lucy? Rosie? Bob?

"Keep your eyes forward and pay attention to what
you're doing, Ma'am." The young policeman shouted.
Ballou yelped, squirming toward his mistress. A gust of
wind brought Kate to her knees. Marlene went down with
her. The bridge swayed. The bridge at St. Luis Rey came
to mind. Several people screamed. Rosie's was the most
riveting. Would they ever get to the other side?

As the evacuees—that's how Kate now defined herself—
settled into the smelly, overcrowded high-school gym, she
figured the misanthrope next door might have had the right
idea. Ocean Vista never looked better. Maybe she should
have stayed in her apartment and taken her chances.

"Could ya believe that bus ride?" Rosie lit a
Chesterfield. "Not even a toilet in the back. Don't they
know us old broads need to pee every hour? And the ladies
room in this school could use a little elbow grease.
Clorox, that's my secret weapon."

"Please put that cigarette out, Ma'am." The young, gal-
lant cop who'd carried Ballou to safety sounded peeved.

Rosie made a face, but dropped the cigarette into her
Coke can.

"If I catch you lighting up again, Ma'am, I'll have to
confiscate your cigarettes." The cop returned to his task at
hand, assigning sleeping quarters. No one wanted the
bleacher benches, but floor space was at a premium.

Kate felt sorry for him. And annoyed at Rosie. They were in a school, for heaven's sake. Why would Rosie think she could smoke? And why did she keep lumping Kate and herself in the same "old broad" category? The former Rockette had been dancing at Radio City before Kate was born. And their age difference put Rosie in a different generation, didn't it? Kate laughed. She'd better stop talking to herself: she sounded exactly like a cranky old broad.

"What's so funny?" Rosie asked, stretching her thin arms to the floor, then walking them around in a circle.

Amazing. Rosie O'Grady smoked like Bette Davis in *Dark Victory*, drank like a sailor on shore leave, had slept with Albert Anastasia, and, if you could believe her, most of the Rat Pack. At eighty-four, she rasped, but remained as limber and healthy as a teenager. So much for clean living.

"Life's funny." Kate sighed. "Would you like a couple of Social Teas? I have a thermos of tea, too."

"Thanks, but no thanks. I have a flask of gin."

"I'll have one of those, young man." Lucy Diamond cornered one of St. Thomas's teenage volunteers handing out pillows and blankets. She pointed to a bunch of cots that would fetch some really big bucks if they went up for bid. "My spine is arthritic and I cannot spend the night on the floor or up in those bleachers."

The boy shook his head. "I'm not fixing to assign the cots, Ma'am. Y'all will have to figure that out."

A Florida native, judging by his accent. A rare breed, displaced by uppity Northerners who'd taken over their towns, not unlike the carpetbaggers during the Reconstruction period after the Civil War.

"I want that cot. " Lucy Diamond, the hard-hitting federal prosecutor, would have given General Sherman pause. "If you hand over two pillows and a blanket, I'll make my bed up now."

The boy took her in stride. "You might want to talk to your condo commander, Ma'am." Not a trace of irony in his voice.

Walt Weatherwise, a two-way transistor radio tucked into his pocket and a pile of bedding clutched under his right arm, used his left index finger to tap the teenager's shoulder. "Do you know who I am, boy?"

The kid stared at Weatherwise, meeting his eyes and not blinking, then shook his head. "I sure don't, mister."

"I'm Uncle Weatherwise, from Channel Eight." The boy's face remained blank. "Your hurricane point man. I'm in contact with the United States Weather Service, receiving updates every five minutes." He kicked the left front metal wheels on one of the remaining cots in the small pile. "I am requisitioning this bed. The bureau has upgraded the hurricane to a Category Two. With my many years of experience and the ongoing input from the Weather Service, I can guide us through Harriet and save our lives." Weatherwise grabbed the cot, propped a pillow up against the gym wall, and stretched out. His feet dangled over its bottom end and his love handles flopped over its sides.

"That's my bed, you old fraud. Get up." Lucy, who'd stood by brooding, lashed out at Weatherwise.

"What are you going to do, put me in jail?" A smiling Uncle used his soothing, trained-for-television voice.

The kid caved. "You can each have a cot." He set up Lucy's as far away from Weatherwise as the geography would allow, then walked toward the cafeteria.

The wind whistled through the gym's closed windows.

Rain seeped through a rear window. Kate thought she felt the school move. Ballou, who'd been off exploring, returned to her side and licked her hand, comforting her.

"Give me the latitude again," Weatherwise barked into his cell phone.

It was going to be a long night.

On the bleacher below her, Marlene snored. Kate had dozed, but Weatherwise haunted her dreams. The ghost of hurricanes past? Why did she dislike him so? She hardly knew him.

"Don't threaten me, Walt. You're in way too deep." Fury coated Bob Seeley's words.

Good lord, why would Bob have been threatening the weatherman? Kate raised her head, straining to hear.

"The money better show up, Bob. By tomorrow." Weatherwise laughed.

Mild-mannered Bob's anger had shocked Kate, but Weatherwise's evil laugh scared her.

All that rage had to stem from something deeper than condo finances. Something from the men's past?

How she wished she could roll over.

Ballou, thank heavens, was sound asleep. She closed her eyes.

Minutes—hours?—later, Kate awoke again. Sitting up, she spotted Rosie and Weatherwise under the basketball hoop. Rosie, so proud of her high kicks, had wrapped her left leg around his neck. The weatherman squirmed, struggling to remove her ankle, but the octogenarian, in far better shape, just kept on talking. Kate tried, but couldn't make out Rosie's monologue.

•　　•　　•

Weatherwise must have slipped out while the weary slept.

At seven the next morning, no one seemed to care. And no one seemed to care that most of the hurricane hype had been just that.

Harriet, downgraded to a tropical storm, had hit Palmetto Beach at two A.M., then veered south.

The power was back on, sunshine streamed through the gym's windows, and Channel Eight's substitute weatherman, all smiles, announced there had been no reported injuries and property damage was being assessed.

Ocean Vista's residents, following a flurry of loud conversations, had demanded to go home to see for themselves.

Kate wiped her face with a Wash'n Dri and took Ballou for a walk. The buses would be picking them up in an hour.

Piles of debris were scattered in front of the school. Ballou investigated them thoroughly, sniffing each and every one. After he'd done his business and Kate had used her pooper-scooper, he returned to one of the higher piles.

"Come on Ballou, we have a bus to catch."

The Westie ignored her, digging deeper, exposing part of a large black plastic bag.

Could that be the toe of a sneaker sticking out? She peered closer. Yes, for sure—a Nike, covering a foot. Using her own sneaker, she kicked away the bag, revealing the rest of Uncle Weatherwise.

Four

A weather vane had pierced his heart.

The killer must have sharpened the vane's east arrow into a weapon. Kate, feeling sick, moved in closer. That would make Uncle Weatherwise's death premeditated murder.

A homicide detective's widow, Kate had shared decades of deadly pillow talk with Charlie and knew that Weatherwise couldn't have been dead for long. She glanced at her watch. A little after seven. She'd guess three hours at the most.

Though his florid face had lost its color, if it weren't for the surprisingly small amount of blood around the wound, the weatherman might be sleeping. Naked except for bold red plaid boxers with a Ralph Lauren label, the corpse sported a slight smile. Or maybe a sneer. Uncle Weatherwise's smile had often seemed like a sneer.

Once again, a sense of déjà vu swept over Kate.

Another man with a smile like a sneer. Who? For a fleeting second, she thought she remembered, then the image vanished.

She dialed 911. When no one answered after six rings, she hung up. The 911 operators must be flooded with calls on the morning after a hurricane.

Kate bit the bullet and called Nick Carbone. If he referenced Miss Marple, she'd just have to kill him.

"Carbone." Nick's gruff voice sounded as rude as ever. Somehow that comforted her. She'd reached the stage of life where she really didn't like change.

"It's Kate Kennedy, Nick."

"I just called you, your cell phone was busy." He coughed. Embarrassed? "Wanted to see if you were okay. Did you evacuate?"

Damn the man. Why didn't he ever call when things were okay? Whoa, Kate. Did she really want him to call? Maybe.

"Yes, we were evacuated. I'm calling from St. Thomas High School in Coral Reef. Most of Ocean Vista slept here last night."

"Good. Glad you're safe. I hear the beach is a real mess."

"I have a bit of a mess out here."

"Oh?" Nick sounded less than interested.

She glanced over at the dead man. A seagull was circling him. Kate had never seen one this far west. The weatherman's whale-like white belly exposed above the expensive designer drawers saddened her. She walked back to Weatherwise's body and, though probably tampering with evidence, bent and re-covered his remains with the garbage bag. Then she fumbled in her pocket for a Wash'n Dri.

"Kate?"

"Sorry, Nick, I was just protecting the corpse from the hot sun."

Though his jurisdiction ended at Palmetto Beach's western border, Nick Carbone appeared on the scene less than fifteen minutes later.

Sure that no one would be going anywhere, Kate had decided not to tell anyone—not even Marlene—about the murder until either Nick, the Coral Reef homicide detectives, or the bus that would transport the Ocean Vista residents back home arrived. She wasn't surprised when Carbone got there first.

Kate had planned to use those fifteen minutes to observe the suspects—she never even considered an outsider might be the perpetrator—while the killer still believed the body hadn't been discovered.

She'd forgotten that the best laid plans can go astray. Suspect number one, Rosie O'Grady, hosted an impromptu dance party and supects two and three were eager participants. A CD in Bob's laptop provided the music: the Andrews Sisters. Rosie sang along as she swung out and in of Joe Sajak's arms.

Bob's long legs had moved with the grace of the old movie musical hoofer, Dan Daily. Kate thought he looked a bit like the actor, too. Who'd have thought refined, stodgy old Bob could perform such a great Lindy Hop? But then who'd have thought Uncle Weatherwise would be threatening the condo's finance chair about missing money?

Lucy Diamond, her dark pageboy bouncing, had partnered with a new owner, a younger guy—only in South

Florida could fifty-five be considered young—from the first
floor. He hustled to keep up with the retired prosecutor.

Marlene had grabbed Kate and they danced together
like the teenagers they once were, the steps coming easy
as Marlene led. Kate remembered Marlene had taught
Charlie to dance, too.

No one seemed to miss the weatherman. Not even
Kate, the dancing detective.

Nick Carbone had cut in. He didn't look happy as he
swung Kate out, saying, "Show me the body."

In the blazing sunshine, Kate pointed to the black plastic
bag, wondering if the killer had watched them leave the
dance floor. When Nick had arrived, Marlene mumbled a
puzzled "What's up?" The others, absorbed in dancing
and/or themselves, appeared not to notice.

Nick dropped to his knees and bared the body. He still
favored his left leg, injured in a fall in Broward General
Hospital, slipping on spilled water that Kate hadn't prop-
erly wiped up. "Coral Reef's homicide guys will be here
soon. I just thought I'd take a look."

"How much of a head start did you give yourself,
Nick?" Kate didn't even try to cover her laughter.

"The weather vane intrigues me," Nick said, without
glancing up at her. "Someone making a point."

She laughed again. One of Detective Carbone's few
charms: dry humor. "Uncle Weatherwise called this hurricane wrong, but I don't think Harriet's the motive."

Nick, using the ground as leverage, pushed himself up
and onto his feet. It took some effort. And heavy breathing. Why hadn't he retired? He was only a few years
younger than Kate. Well, maybe more than a few. The

man had no life. Only death, which, like Charlie, he loved to investigate. At least Charlie had Kate and the boys. Nick had no one. Or did he?

Nick smiled, a sly, not a friendly, smile. "Do tell me, Miss Marple, whodunit?"

She wished she had a weapon. "I don't know; however, I do know that three of Ocean Vista's condo board members appear to have motives."

"So a condo commander killed Uncle Weatherwise? Now, really, Jane, er, Kate . . ."

A police siren shut him up.

Five

"Nobody's going nowhere. So settle down, folks." Lee Parker drawled.

The Coral Reef homicide detective and Nick Carbone had conferred for a few minutes and were now standing under the home team's basket, flanked by several policemen in really spiffy uniforms, much nicer than Palmetto Beach's finest.

Kate could see—Mr. Magoo could see—that Nick couldn't stand his counterpart. A study in contrasts. Nick, a brassy Brooklyn transplant, overweight and overbearing. Lee, a lanky, down-home boy, with a master's in art history from the University of Miami, had decided to serve his city by putting the bad guys in their place: jail or the cemetery.

The assembled Ocean Vista residents stirred: restless, puzzled, anxious, and angry.

Ballou, curled up in a corner, slept through the commotion.

"You need to tell us why we're being detained, Detective." Lucy sounded adversarial, probably a mistake, based on Lee Parker's crossed arms and stone face. The former prosecutor pointed to the unhappy bus driver who was pacing in front of the gym door, twirling his hat. "We have to get back to Palmetto Beach. As bylaws chair of Ocean Vista, I demand an explanation for this delay."

"Would a murder investigation suffice, Ms. Diamond?" Detective Parker asked. "Walt Weatherwise is dead. Please take a seat in the bleachers."

Lucy staggered, then murmured, "I wondered where he'd disappeared to." She sank down onto a bench in the front row. "How? When?" Staring into space, she didn't seem to expect an answer.

Kate scanned the crowd, trying to catch Rosie and Bob's reaction.

"The mob!" Rosie, steel-gray curls bouncing, pushed her way in front of an ashen Joe Sajak. "A hit, right? The New York wiseguys iced Weatherwise. I ain't a bit surprised; he had it coming."

"I'm off, then," Nick extended his hand to Lee Parker. "Call me if I can be of any help." He left without even a good-bye nod to Kate.

Feeling abandoned, she realized she'd counted on Nick being there when Detective Parker interviewed her. Now she was on her own.

"Everyone, please take a seat." Detective Parker spoke in a low voice, polite as a hostess at a backyard barbecue, but no one could mistake his request for anything less than an order. "Officers Logan and Bernstein will be recording all your names and phone numbers. Your condo units, too."

Parker ignored the crowd's grumbling and groans, and gestured toward Kate. "Mrs. Kennedy, I'd like to ask you a few questions."

Butterflies flooded her digestive tract, flying both ways. Did she have a Pepcid AC in her pocket? Relax. After all, Nick must have told Parker she'd discovered the body. It wasn't as if she'd killed Uncle Weatherwise. Though she couldn't have felt any more nervous if she had.

"Let's grab a cup of coffee from the refreshment table," Parker said.

She trailed behind him to a metal table covered with a white cloth, Thermoses of coffee and tea, bottled water, muffins, other goodies that the St. Thomas High School Boosters Club had provided for the evacuees.

Parker poured and handed her a mug of coffee. "Here you go, little lady." The detective smiled down at her in the benevolent despot tone and manner that many younger men in positions of authority use when addressing elderly—or what they perceive to be elderly—women.

"I drink tea, Detective Parker." Assertive, not aggressive. "And I can pour my own, thank you." She reached across him, lifted the tea Thermos, and filled a mug without a visible shake or spill, though the butterflies were drag-racing through her esophagus.

She had no appetite; the gym smelled of sweat, and even with the air conditioner on, she felt clammy.

"Muffin, Mrs. Kennedy?" None too sharp about body language, was he?

"No, thank you." Were they just going to keep standing here? She'd be damned if she'd suggest sitting.

"Okay, let's take it from the top, Ma'am." Parker paused, sipped his coffee, and stared at her, waiting.

She added a smidgen of milk, stirred for a long time, and smiled up at him, trying for guileless. And clueless.

"You were out walking your dog, right?"

Silent, hoping to appear to be in deep reflection, Kate nodded. If she only had a Pepcid AC, she'd almost be enjoying herself.

"And," Parker prompted, "what did you see, Mrs. Kennedy?"

"See?" She shook her head. "I don't quite understand your question."

"Now, look here," the detective sputtered, sending spittle into the space between them.

Kate stepped to the right, out of range. "Well, at least at first, all I saw were piles of debris. Ballou discovered the body."

"Since I can't interview your dog, Mrs. Kennedy, please speak for him." Parker sounded as if his patience had run out.

"Ballou uncovered a large black plastic bag, then investigated, sniffing away. I noticed a sneaker—a Nike—protruding out from under the bag and went over for a better look."

"And?"

"A foot was in the sneaker."

"What did you do then, Mrs. Kennedy?" Exasperation punctuated his question.

"I kicked away the rest of the bag and exposed Walt Weatherwise's body."

"How did you know he was dead?"

"A weather vane had pierced his heart." Kate felt no obligation to discuss either her decades of pillow talk with the best homicide detective in New York City or the growing number of dead bodies she'd encountered since moving to Palmetto Beach.

"How were you so sure that Weatherwise hadn't been badly injured but still alive?"

Tempted to tell the chauvinist "women's intuition," instead Kate shrugged and said, "I don't know how I knew, I just did."

The expression on Lee Parker's face could only be described as disgust. "Did you touch the body or any part of the crime scene?"

Oh God. Had Nick told this condescending lout that she'd covered the corpse?

"Mrs. Kennedy, answer my question. Did you disturb the body or the crime scene?"

"Kate, don't answer that." Lucy Diamond's court-trained voice boomed out from behind. The former prosecutor thrust herself between Parker and Kate, wagging her index finger in Parker's direction. "Is Mrs. Kennedy a suspect, Detective?"

The butterflies reached Kate's throat. If she hadn't been a suspect before, she'd bet she was one now.

SIX

"Maybe Lucy killed him," Marlene whispered to Kate. "You know, pretending to defend and protect you, while planting suspicion. Devious, but clever, right?"

The last to board, they sat in the back of the fourth and final of the St. Thomas school buses to leave the gym. Ballou settled in on Auntie Marlene's lap and snored. Assorted cats, dogs, birds, Rosie O'Grady's bunny rabbit, and Bob Seeley's white mice in a Calvin Klein shoe box had inspired Marlene to nickname the bus Noah's Wheels.

Competing animal cries filled the narrow aisle and Noah's Wheels smelled like the monkey cage in the Central Park Zoo. Kate, certain her aroma was as bad as the pets, tried—and failed—to pry open a dirt-crusted window. She popped a Pepcid AC and two Tylenols followed by an Evian chaser.

More than the stench bothered her. When the driver had yelled, "All aboard, last call for Ocean Vista!" Lee Parker had *invited* Kate to stop by his office later that afternoon. Lucy Diamond, still in the detective's face, had volunteered to come along.

Lucy now sat two rows in front of Kate and Marlene, cuddling her Siamese cat, and shouting legal advice to Kate over Bob's bald head.

"Knock it off, Lucy," Marlene shouted back, then turned to Kate. "That woman's setting you up as prime suspect."

Kate, haunted by Weatherwise's face, squirmed, but said nothing. A shiver spread over her, leaving a chill in its wake. A blast from the past? A buried memory?

"Kate, did you hear me?" Marlene sounded so far away. Kate tuned her out.

Why did Uncle Weatherwise seem familiar? She'd seldom watched him on the Channel Eight News and had never laid eyes on him in the flesh until he arrived at Ocean Vista.

The Pepcid AC went to work and Kate felt better. She opened her eyes and sat up straight.

"Are you okay?" An edge of anger coated Marlene's concern.

"Yes, don't worry. I'm just tired." Kate lied. She smiled at Marlene. "We'll be home soon."

"God knows what havoc Mother Nature has wrought," Marlene groaned. "We'll deal with that later." She leaned closer to Kate. "Don't let Lucy come with us this afternoon."

"Us?"

"Well, you're not planning on seeing Parker without me, are you?"

Kate laughed, patting Marlene's hand. "No, but I am

planning on avoiding Lucy until you and I return from Coral Reef's Police Department."

Bold, bright sunshine as they crossed the bridge to A1A belied their dark and miserable journey west the night before. The pastel stucco stores and restaurants lining both sides of Neptune Boulevard appeared intact, if water stained, and cluttered with flotsam and jetsam up to their doorknobs. Straight ahead on the otherwise deserted beach, a crew from the Palmetto Beach Parks Department swept up debris and raked the sand. Good to see their tax dollars, at the third highest rate per capita in Broward County, being put to good use.

A1A was empty. No traffic. No people. Just the little yellow school bus winding its way up Ocean Vista's circular driveway and depositing its weary evacuees at the condo's imposing front door. Be it ever so grandiose, there's no place like home.

A flashback to her childhood home in Queens, a red brick semi-attached, two-family—far from fancy—house with a forest-green door and shutters and a wide brick stoop with a low wall separating it from the house next door, popped into Kate's head. A smiling Uncle Weatherwise opened the front door. She screamed.

"Good God, what's wrong?" Marlene's shout bounced Kate out of the past.

Lucy, standing in line to exit the bus, swung around, almost dropping Anna, her sleek, black Siamese. "Don't let your nerves get the better of you, Kate. A witness in a murder investigation must remain calm and collected. And, of course, I'll be at your side during the interrogation with Detective Parker, so you have nothing to fear."

But fear itself, Kate thought, as she held out her arm to keep Marlene at bay.

"Let me at her," Marlene snarled through clenched teeth.

"Later." Kate sounded as shaky as she felt. "Let's assess the damage and have lunch first."

The wall-to-wall carpet was ruined, but Kate had never liked it much anyway. Her son Peter's partner, Edmund, a plastic surgeon by trade and an interior decorator by design, had used a white and off-white palette throughout the entire apartment, too neutral and too sterile even for Kate. She'd rip up the Berber and replace it with terracotta tile. Add a little warmth to her life. The legs on the oak dining room table and chairs would have to be restained; however, the rest of the inside damage appeared to be minimal.

She stepped outside and into a pool of muddy water. Her plants were ruined and many of their pots had been smashed to smithereens. Clean-up could wait till tomorrow. Since most everything else on the balcony was plastic, she wouldn't have to replace the table and chairs. Marlene, who used her ground-floor balcony as an extra closet, would not fare so well.

Kate breathed in the sweet ocean air, considering herself and her neighbors very lucky. She wondered if the misanthrope next door had been disappointed.

The Palmetto Beach Parks Department had already replaced the lifeguard station. The wreckage of the old one lay to its left, waiting to be loaded into an orange dump truck, looked just like Kevin's favorite childhood toy.

At the rate the workers were moving, by tomorrow the beach would be restored to its former glory.

Miss Mitford—who'd manned the front desk ever since

Ocean Vista first opened—had advised the bedraggled owners that there was running water and the electric power had been restored an hour ago. Had the sentinel ever left her post? Nah. Knowing Mitford, she'd slept in the lobby last night—like Kate's neighbor—prepared to go down with the condo.

Her damage inspection over and her to-do list complete, Kate headed for the kitchen to make a nice cup of tea.

By noon, with the ruined carpet rolled into a corner and the water mopped up, Kate the Capable, as Marlene had dubbed her sister-in-law decades ago, was walking Ballou on Neptune Boulevard. Only mad dogs, Englishmen, and South Florida Westie owners go out in the midday sun. Though she'd showered and washed her hair, Kate was drenched in sweat, her blue T-shirt clinging to her bra.

Several shop owners were taking down the wooden boards and masking tape they'd swathed across their doors and windows the evening before. Looked like tough going, but the beauty salon was already open for business.

Kate nodded to the owner of Dinah's, her favorite coffee shop, one of the few restaurants in Broward County where a small dog could sit at his mistress's feet while she enjoyed poached eggs and whole-wheat toast slathered with homemade strawberry jam.

"Come on, Ballou," Kate said, pulling him in the opposite direction, aiming east toward the beach. "Let's go see how the pier and the Neptune Inn weathered the storm."

If the Inn were open, she'd bring a couple of cheeseburgers home for her and Marlene's lunch.

"Psst! Kate."

Her mind on the upcoming homicide interrogation, she wasn't sure that someone had spoken. Ballou's yelp convinced her. She spun around.

Standing in Mancini's doorway—the restaurant was still boarded up—Bob grabbed her arm. "Kate," his voice cracked, "you have to help me. I know who murdered Uncle Weatherwise."

"Who?"

"Rosie O'Grady."

seven

"Are you going to tell Detective Parker what Bob Seeley said?"

The top of Marlene's white '57 Chevy convertible was down, and a mild summer breeze, a lingering residue from last night's hurricane, rippled through Kate's hair, but didn't make a dent in her sister-in-law's French twist. The sun shone bright and beautiful above a landscape marred with bags of trash and mounds of debris. They were on Neptune Boulevard heading west to the Coral Reef Police Department.

"Why do you suppose they named the town Coral Reef? It's more than twenty miles away from the Atlantic."

Marlene huffed. "Like Oceanside, Long Island, is on the ocean? Don't change the subject, Kate." She went through a yellow light starting to turn red. "You don't want to conceal evidence in a murder investigation, do you?"

Kate, stumped, sighed.

"You have to tell Parker."

"I don't know if I believe Bob. Think about it, Marlene." Kate counted on her fingers, starting with the pinkie. "One—Bob tells me he saw a weather vane sticking out of Rosie's tote bag the night before the murder. Last night. Somehow it seems like ages ago." Kate moved to her index finger. "Two—the weather vane had gone missing when Bob rummaged through her bag on the bus ride home; the first opportunity he'd had to check it out after hearing about the murder."

"Well, of course the weather vane went missing from the bag, Kate. It was stuck in Weatherwise's heart."

Kate, on a roll, tapped her middle finger. "Three—even if Bob's telling the truth, why would Rosie have left the murder weapon sticking out of her own tote bag for all the evacuees to see?"

"But why would dear, dull old Bob lie like that?" Marlene jerked her head around to face Kate. "You don't think *Bob* murdered Uncle Weatherwise, do you?"

"Maybe." Kate shrugged . "Or maybe the killer planted the weapon in Rosie's bag, hoping someone, anyone, would notice it. And remember it. Maybe the killer—and, yes, it might be Bob—then removed the weather vane before dawn." Kate started. "Marlene you just ran a red light right in front of the police station."

The young cop who issued the moving violation ticket appeared hot and unhappy. When Marlene tried to fob off her offense, explaining they'd been running late for Kate's

appointment with Lee Parker, the cop flushed scarlet.
"The courthouse is right around the corner, Ma'am. You
can follow me over there now and pay your fine while
your friend here chats with Detective Parker."

So Kate, standing as tall as her sixty-three inches
would stretch, went solo into the pastel pink stucco Coral
Reef Police Department. The courthouse was a deeper
shade, almost quartz. Lots of pink and coral going on in
this town, a wannabe Boca.

The lobby had a Spanish flair, too. Dark wood furniture
and terra-cotta tiles—the floor would look great in her
condo. Taxpayers' dollars had provided a warm welcome
for the good, the bad, and the ugly—plus their attorneys—
who sat waiting to be called. Coral Reef citizens could afford to be cavalier; they had the second highest income
per capita in Broward County.

A young, pretty woman in a well-pressed uniform took
Kate's name and entered it in a log. "Please have a seat,
Mrs. Kennedy. Detective Parker will be with you soon."

Kate sat, pulled out her blue notebook, and mused over
motives. Lucy Diamond and Uncle Weatherwise had quar-
reled over the planting of medicinal marijuana, but their
nasty exchange at the shelter led Kate to believe that Lucy
and Walt must have crossed paths prior to Ocean Vista.
Maybe years ago in Miami, long before Kate, or even
Marlene, had moved to South Florida. Could Walt have
been in trouble with the Feds? Could Lucy have prosecuted him? Easy enough to check. Kate starred an entry.

Fifteen minutes passed. "Soon"—iffy at best. The
good, the bad, and the ugly—and their attorneys—had all
been called. Where was Marlene? Had they put her in jail?

"Detective Parker shouldn't be much longer, Ma'am."
The young policewoman spoke without conviction.

Kate returned to her notes. Uncle Weatherwise had threatened docile Bob Seeley, even more mild-mannered than Clark Kent, over some mysterious missing money. A business deal gone sour? Or something more sinister? A motive for murder?

Rosie O'Grady filled an entire page. The dancer's leg wrapped around Weatherwise's neck under the basket remained a vivid image, defying description. The Albert Anastasia connection rang true. Rosie might be misinformed, but Kate was convinced that the former Rockette really believed Uncle Weatherwise had mob ties. Could Rosie have stabbed Weatherwise in a decades-delayed revenge for Anastasia's hit in the Park Sheraton's barbershop?

Walt Weatherwise had raised his arm in a threatening gesture on the bridge. Kate wrote in caps: WHO'D CROSSED BEHIND HIM?

A memory stirred, almost surfaced, then receded. What? Damn it. What? Something Rosie said? Weatherwise on the bridge? The Park Sheraton Hotel? Images whirled in her head. Her notebook slid to the floor; its blue cover clashing with the terra-cotta tile.

"Kate, are you okay? Let me pick that up for you." Lucy Diamond sounded annoyingly solicitous.

What the devil was she doing here? Kate hadn't answered her phone and Marlene had ducked out Ocean Vista's back door, checked out the parking lot, then picked Kate up in front of the lobby to keep Lucy from finding out that they'd left for Coral Reef.

She fell to her knees, grabbing the notebook just as Lucy reached for it, but missed.

"Is that your diary, Kate? I swear I had no intention of

peeking. You've made it clear you don't want me involved." Lucy straightened up and laughed.

Kate resented Lucy's superior snicker. She probably always had, but never more than at this moment. "Why are you here, Lucy?" She stood, clutching the notebook.

"Reviewing the case with Detective Parker. Coral Reef isn't Miami, you know. I offered my expertise." Lucy's tone indicated her offer had been refused.

"Mrs. Kennedy," the policewoman called out. "Detective Parker is ready for you."

Parker's office, filled with framed pictures of himself and laminated *Sun-Sentinel* stories featuring his name above the lead, resembled a nonthinking man's den. Nary a book in sight. And this guy had a master's in art history? The four bookcases were being used as file cabinets. Detective Parker must be a paper person. She'd bet those folders held every scrap of information on every case he'd ever worked.

The walls, or what Kate could see of them—since all four were brag walls—were institutional green that, like her notebook, clashed with the terra-cotta tile. His desk stood in the center of the room; its phone, computer, fax, and printer wires running like eels across the floor to scattered baseboard outlets.

Parker didn't stand. He gestured to a club chair in front of his desk. "Sit down, Mrs. Kennedy."

She did, primly, her back straight, keeping her knees together like the Catholic schoolgirl she'd once been.

His eyes, dark and angry, met hers. Then he picked up a sheet of paper and waved it in her direction. "Out of the past, Mrs. Kennedy." Parker sounded angry. And something more. Cruel. "We're all the sum total of our past lives, aren't we?"

Whatever she'd expected, it hadn't been anything like this. Had Parker gone mad?

She held his gaze, saying nothing.

Parker pushed back his heavy oak chair, walked to the front of his desk, then stood, towering over her. He shifted the piece of paper from one large hand to the other. "Tell me about the summer of 1950, Mrs. Kennedy. The year you turned thirteen."

She shivered and, though she tried not to, she looked away, staring down at the terra-cotta tile.

Kate had few secrets. Her life was an open book . . . except for a brief chapter in the summer of 1950.

Eight

Thursday, June 29, 1950

"Come on, Mom, please. I'll be the only girl at Marlene's house without a bra. You can't do this to me. I'll die of mortification."

Her mother smiled. Kate hoped that was a twinkle in Maggie Norton's blue eyes. Though she could wheedle almost anything out of her mother, this would be a tough sell. Maggie had been a flapper and prided herself on never having worn—or needed—a bra. And even worse, her mother still thought of Kate as a child.

"Mortification, huh? That would be an awful way to go." Maggie sipped her chocolate ice-cream soda, then dipped her long spoon into the tall glass, scooping up the last of the foam.

They were finishing lunch at the counter in the restaurant on the seventh floor of Bloomingdale's. Kate's favorite department store. She hated it when her mother shopped downtown at Orbach's or Klein's, embarrassed that they had to carry the lower priced stores' shopping bags onto the subway.

She'd overheard her mother telling her grandmother, Etta, that Kate was a snob. Her grandmother had just laughed, the way grandmothers, easier-going than mothers, often seemed to do.

"Etta thinks I'm ready for a bra." Kate whispered to her mother in the crowded elevator. Thank God her father, really strict and almost never easygoing, would not be consulted about anything so intimate as a bra.

"Maybe, maybe not," her mother said as they rode down, passing the fourth and third floors with none of the passengers getting off.

"Second Floor: Ladies Lingerie," the elevator operator announced, sounding a lot like the announcer on *The Shadow*, Kate's all-time favorite radio show. He opened the brass gate. A woman in a blue straw hat with a white feather, standing in front of Kate, stepped out.

Her mother poked her in the back. "Get off, Kate, before the gate closes and I change my mind."

Marlene and Kate had been *forever* friends since they were six. And Marlene, always the more daring, had been wearing bras for at least three months. She now owned a collection of five, including a pointy black lace–and–nylon concoction. No wonder Pete Blake, Kate's new neighbor and current crush, seemed so interested in Marlene. If she kept flirting with Pete, Marlene might be in danger of losing her *forever* friend.

After ten minutes of browsing with her mother, Kate

figured she didn't have a prayer of bringing home an exciting or even a pretty bra, but anything would be better than her undershirt. Even the plain white cotton triple-A bra her mother was inspecting.

Her father had ordered an oil burner to replace their coal stove. To celebrate the last heat to emanate from the old furnace, Kate would love to have a bonfire of undershirts. She'd throw in her seven-days-of-the-week underpants, too. Not to mention her scapula.

On this, her thirteenth birthday, to her amazement and delight, Kate got to pick out her own presents. Very much a woman of the world, like her namesake, Katharine Hepburn, in *Adam's Rib*.

Kate went home with three bras—one pink and edged with embroidery, two white, trimmed with lace—and six pairs of darling pastel panties, all wrapped in tissue paper, then folded neatly into her very own Bloomingdale's shopping bag.

She felt very New York City riding the IRT out to Queens. But what a tragedy: no one but her mother and grandmother would ever get to see her pretty new underwear.

"Surprise!" Marlene yelled, the loudest of the crowd in her finished basement.

They'd fooled her. No one, not Mom, Dad, Etta, or Marlene had slipped. Kate stood on the top step of the staircase, staring down, feeling more tricked than pleased. A little voice scolded her. Great, her conscience sounded like her grandmother.

She descended the stairs, smiling, not a bright smile,

but probably okay in the dim light of the finished basement.

"A den," Marlene's mother had dubbed it years ago, pointing to the fireplace they built when they'd redone the cellar. "A place for our family and friends to gather."

Mrs. Friedman wore a satin sheath and a black boa. Kate would bet *her* bra screamed "exciting."

Kate couldn't look at the deer head prominently displayed on the pine wall behind Mr. Friedman's bar. The one time she had, its eyes had held hers and wouldn't let go. Had Marlene's father shot the deer? She'd been afraid to ask.

"What a pretty dress, Kate. You're lovely tonight. Quite the young lady." Mrs. Friedman had a throaty voice, like Lizbeth Scott, the blonde B-movie star, a pale imitation of Lauren Bacall. Kate wondered if Mrs. Friedman, a fashion maven, had noticed her new-and-improved profile.

Fussing over Kate's chestnut curls, her mother had insisted that Kate wear the blue sundress. "The color turns your eyes turquoise, Kate."

Her mom sounded devious. Were all women devious? Would it be better to stay a girl?

Maggie had encouraged Kate to put on a light coat of Cherries in the Snow lipstick, then rubbed some rouge on her cheeks. So why wasn't Kate happy? She had on her pink bra and matching underpants. Her sandals had a low wedge that made her appear a little taller, and even her father had said she looked nice. High praise from him.

Could thirteen be a turning point? Maybe she'd never be happy again.

"Kate," Mrs. Friedman said, embracing her. "Welcome to womanhood."

Over Marlene's mother's shoulder, Kate met the deer's left eye. She'd swear he was winking at her.

She slow danced to "Mona Lisa" with Robby Carruthers—one of Marlene's discards—who would be starting his freshman year at Regis High School in the fall. Too old and too tall for Kate, Robby didn't even try to hide his boredom.

Mrs. Friedman put out the food on two side-by-side metal card tables covered with pink cloths and decorated with HAPPY BIRTHDAY balloons. Each crystal plate and bowl had a small, printed sign—like a place card— propped up in front of it: "Chicken Salad." "Macaroni Salad." And something called "Tomato Surprise." Lots of good breads, including marble rye, one of Kate's favorites. And a huge platter of homemade "Chocolate and Walnut Brownies."

"Eat!" Mrs. Friedman ordered. "Birthday cake and ice cream will be served later."

The Friedmans filled their plates, then went upstairs to the living room to watch *The Million Dollar Movie*. The television show's instantly recognized music, "Tara's Theme" from *Gone With the Wind*, could be heard loud and clear in the basement.

Marlene winked, and ran up the stairs, shouting, "I'm closing the door, Mom. That music's too loud."

The games began.

The spinning bottle missed Kate three times in a row. When it finally pointed her way, she had to kiss bad-breath Barry. The crowd moved on to "Let's Play Post Office."

By the time Marlene's mother reappeared and switched the overhead light back on, she found several couples necking in dark corners.

Pete Blake and Marlene, unseen by Kate, had squeezed into the broom closet. When an angry Mrs. Freidman jerked the door open, Marlene's black bra was draped around Pete's neck.

How could Marlene have betrayed her? She knew how much Kate liked Pete Blake. And Marlene had tons of boys after her and her 38 C bra. Kate's *forever* friend had behaved like a traitor. Like Alger Hiss. Kate vowed to never speak to her again.

Nine

Monday, July 3, 1950

Over the next few days, the United States Army marched into Korea, Pete moved on to blonder pastures, and Kate met Marlene's possible replacement in Miss Ida's bookstore.

Jackson Heights, though in Queens—one of the five boroughs that made up New York City—suffered, in Kate's opinion, from small-town syndrome. Yes, riding the IRT or the E or F train she could get to Times Square in under a half hour, faster than many Manhattan residents living down in Little Italy or up in Harlem could, but a real Manhattanite didn't have to cross a bridge or tunnel to arrive at Forty-second Street. And nothing exciting ever happened in Jackson Heights.

Except for the growing number of high-rises and the density of the population, she might as well have been living in Kansas City. Well, maybe Philadelphia. But for sure, sophistication began at York Avenue and ended at Twelfth, the east and west boundaries of the city she loved. Forget about neighbors' goods or wives, what Kate coveted was a brownstone on the Upper East Side.

She'd learned as a toddler that Eighty-ninth Street in Jackson Heights was very different from East Eighty-ninth or West Eighty-ninth in the city. Her parents considered their Queens lifestyle a big step up; Kate considered it an embarrassment. She'd rather live in Hell's Kitchen where her father had grown up. The script played out: poor, but brilliant girl goes to Columbia on a scholarship, then marries a boy from Sutton Place. Very Gene Tierney. Or Harlem, where her mother had grown up. That plot line included helping disadvantaged children, working with church groups, and falling in love with a doctor. Very Jeanne Crain.

Stuck in Queens, she'd turned to the society page in the *Journal-American* to fuel her fantasies. Cholly Knickerbocker's column had captured her interest six months ago, and know she couldn't go a day without gossip about the rich and famous.

The columnist's real name was Igor Cassini, a Russian emigre, and the brother of Oleg Cassini, the fashion designer married to Gene Tierney. Such great stuff that she'd thought about giving up *Photoplay* and *Modern Screen*. She found old money more intriguing than movie moneymakers. Louella Parsons covered Hollywood, and Dorothy Kilgallen was the *Voice of Broadway*. Far better than most fan magazines.

On Saturday, her father had laughed when he came out of the ocean and discovered Kate sitting in his beach chair, soaking up the sun and the *Journal-American*'s editorial page at Rockaway Beach.

She loved the writers: Pegler, Pearson, Durling, and Jim Bishop. Such conflict, so much diversity, all on one page. Her mother, already nagging Kate about dropping Marlene, hadn't been amused. "Bill, your daughter is now addicted to politics as well as gossip."

Her father had shrugged. "It's all the same."

Kate was, indeed, fascinated by, if not addicted to, one story. A spy case. The events leading up to the impending arrest of Julius Rosenberg for spying had been making the Hearst paper's headlines for months. All the columnists seemed to agree his wife, Ethel, might be arrested, too. The couple's pictures—two ordinary people who could be Kate's neighbors—had been featured on the *Journal-American*'s front page almost every day.

With the *Daily News* and Walter Winchell in the *Mirror* also required reading, Kate found less time for her first love, books.

Still, on the day before the Fourth of July, she walked the block and a half to Thirty-seventh Avenue to pick up the new *Beverly Gray* mystery. Miss Ida had called early this morning to inform her favorite customer, Maggie Norton, that Kate's special order had arrived.

The bookstore, on the west side of the avenue, sandwiched between the Castle Cave, the bar on the corner, and the dry cleaners, had been Kate's favorite place to hang out prior to her spending most afternoons sipping egg creams at Irv's, a candy store on the east corner, where the boys were.

"Katie, it's wonderful to see you." Miss Ida, prim in a high neck white blouse, despite the summer heat and a store cooled by two fans almost as old as the proprietor, stood behind the counter arranging a display rack of recently released hard cover rentals. "So grown-up you are. So pretty in your pink shirt."

Kate felt herself flush, hot red spreading from neck to temple. She stared down at the floor, mumbling, "Thank you." Her legs looked stumpy in her Bermuda shorts. And her toes, that her mother had painted in Revlon's Fire & Ice stuck too far out of her white sandals.

The tiny bookstore's lending library did a brisk business. Maggie Norton, a loyal customer, had never liked being wait-listed for months at the Jackson Heights Branch of the New York City Public Library. For ten cents a day, Maggie and her neighbors could read the new releases while the books were still on the *Times'* bestseller list.

Kate had orders to pick up a copy of *The Cardinal* that her mother had reserved weeks in advance. She placed a five dollar bill on the counter. "How are you, Miss Ida? Mom says, 'Hi.'"

Miss Ida, bracketed by three walls filled with books, reached under the old oak countertop and, with a flourish, placed the latest *Beverly Gray* in front of Kate.

Another love lost. The thrill of seeing, feeling, smelling a hot-off-the-printing-press mystery in the girl-reporter series had vanished. Poof. Gone. Just like that.

Had Kate become fickle? Tossing old friends away? First, Marlene, leaving her flat, after having been best friends for more than half of their lifetimes. Now, Beverly. Their love affair had begun with *Beverly Gray, Freshman*. Kate had remained a fan all through the plucky heroines college days, her career, her world cruise, in the Orient, on a treasure hunt, and, of course, her romance. Would Beverly wind up with Larry or Jim?

Frankly, Kate, who'd just read *Gone With the Wind*, didn't give a damn.

"What's wrong, dear?" Miss Ida sounded concerned. "You seem a bit odd, Katie."

"Nothing." Kate nodded toward the now undesired Beverly. "Please put that in a bag, Miss Ida, along with *The Cardinal*."

She fought an urge to flee. From what? Her family? Her choice in literature? Her past? Holy smoke, she'd just turned thirteen! Shouldn't she wait until she was twenty to have a nervous breakdown?

Miss Ida handed Kate two dollars and seventy-five cents change. "Please tell your mother that *Kon-Tiki* is scheduled to be returned tomorrow."

"I'm waiting for that book as well." A refined voice, not a native New Yorker—a rare breed in Queens—came from behind Kate, who hadn't realized anyone else had entered the store.

Kate spun around. The good diction belonged to an exotic, dark-haired, slim girl about Kate's age. She wore blue jeans and a peasant blouse; its embroidery gathered around her small, firm, breasts. No bra. No undershirt. Finding her different, but beautiful, Kate stared at the girl's olive skin and huge, almond-shaped brown eyes.

"Katie, say hello to Sophie Provakov," Miss Ida said. "She loves books as much as you do." The spry eighty-two-year-old smiled. "Sophie, this is Kate Norton."

Sophie nodded, then ignoring Kate, addressed Miss Ida. "Am I not the next reader for *Kon-Tiki*?"

Miss Ida chuckled. "Don't you worry, I have two copies, Sophie dear. Yours is right here." Her slim hand darted under the counter and produced the book in question.

Kate's mood lifted. Sophie, speaking up, intrigued her. Bold. Not a boy. Kate had tried—and failed—boy chasing. And not the same old garden variety neighborhood kind of girl. Not Marlene. Not any of the girls at school. Sophie Provakov. She rolled the foreign-sounding name around in her head. Maybe Russian? Kate's father didn't trust the Soviets. And Senator McCarthy blamed communism for all the world's evil.

No matter. Whatever Sophie's heritage and wherever she now lived, Kate wanted to be her friend.

ten

Monday, July 3, 1950

Fate in the form of their mutual fondness for egg creams played into Kate's hand.

The two girls wound up sitting side by side at the counter in Irv's Candy Store, sipping sodas. Kate took the plunge. "I've never tasted a vanilla egg cream." She stirred chocolate foam, trying to look nonchalant.

"Here, taste mine." Sophie pushed her glass in front of Kate's. The hair on Sophie's bronzed bare arm had been bleached blonde by the sun. Good. She must like the beach.

Though she desperately wanted to, Kate couldn't bring herself to use Sophie's straw. Her overly fastidious mother and her "wear your gloves on the subway at all times in all seasons" grandmother had transmitted their fear of germs. The dilemma made Kate hesitate.

Sophie reached over and pressed the plastic straw dispenser. "Use this." She seemed amused, not annoyed.

Kate nodded. "I know. Weird, right? I'm a third-generation cleanliness freak. My family's into germ warfare."

"I'm an expert in dealing with strange parents, Kate. Would you like to meet my father?" Sophie smiled. "He'll serve you hot tea in a fancy glass."

Would she ever!

In instant *like*, exchanging hopes, dreams, and favorite movie stars—both had crushes on Montgomery Clift— they chattered nonstop for seven blocks. Who needed Marlene? This exotic, smart, almond-eyed girl might become Kate's new best friend.

Sophie lived in an old, rather run-down stucco apartment house directly across Thirty-fourth Avenue from the empty lot where, for a few days every August, a traveling carnival set up rides, poker games, and cotton candy stands, then folded its tents and stole away into the night. Even as a little kid, Kate had sensed the carnival's sleaze.

The rumor mill and the *Long Island Star-Journal* had been reporting that some guy named Trump was thinking about buying up empty lots in the low Nineties between Northern Boulevard and Thirty-fourth Avenue and building several high-rise apartment complexes.

Kate's father had not sounded pleased when he'd explained to her mother why Mr. Trump's proposed project would forever change Jackson Heights's charm. More brick and mortar, fewer lawns and gardens.

Sophie would be one of Kate's few friends who lived in an apartment house.

Kate's grandaunts, her father's aunts and Etta's sisters-in-law, lived with two of their widowed brothers in a huge apartment in an elegant old stone building on Central Park West. She more than coveted the huge dollhouse, bigger than a beach cabana, that the "aunties" had bought for another grandniece who, following her mother's death, also now lived with the four old maids. But that odd mix of Nortons were the only apartment dwellers in the Norton clan.

Sophie's lobby had peeling paint, faded furniture, and an odd, unpleasant aroma. It hung in the air, enveloping and offending. Kate sniffed. Cabbage. Kate's mother boiled cabbage in a big cast-iron pot, together with corned beef and potatoes on St. Patrick's Day. Not Kate's favorite meal, though cabbage tasted somewhat better than it smelled.

"We're on the third floor." Sophie pressed the elevator call button, seemingly oblivious to the odor.

A tall, thin man dressed in shiny black pants and a tattered plaid bathrobe worn over a white undershirt opened the door to apartment 307. "My dear, did you forget again your key? I am in the middle of my work." Sophie's father had an accent like Paul Henreid in *Casablanca*. He even looked a little bit like the actor.

"Father, I have brought home a friend." Kate's heart smiled when Sophie referred to her as a friend. "This is Kate Norton. We met in Miss Ida's bookstore." She turned to Kate. "This is my father, Boris Provakov."

"Well, come in, come in, young ladies, we'll have tea." Mr. Provakov sounded polite, and grinned widely, revealing a gold tooth, but Kate felt certain he found her visit intrusive.

Sophie's father worked at home. A concept so alien that Kate had never heard of, much less met, such a man before. Even more intriguing, Mrs. Provokov went to work every day at a real job in a real office while her husband stayed in the apartment, fixing his daughter's lunch, and preparing tea for her friends.

Carpets hung on the walls. Books were everywhere. In the corner of the living room serving as Mr. Provokov's office, a drafting table was filled with hand-drawn maps and small black notebooks, one of them open, crammed with strange-looking letters of what Sophie called the Cyrillic alphabet.

Mr. Provokov spoke to his daughter in a language that Kate figured had to be Russian and Sophie closed the notebook.

A shortwave radio, its crackles interrupted by staccato sentences—again, in what must be Russian—sat on top of a steel file cabinet with locked doors. While her father brewed tea in the kitchen, Sophie told Kate that Mr. Provokov wore the keys to the cabinet on a chain around his neck. "I warned you my parents were strange."

The sweet tea—no milk—was, indeed, served in tall glasses, not unlike the ones their egg creams had been in, except these glasses were crystal with a fancy design and sterling silver holders.

Strange or not, Kate found herself liking Mr. Provokov, who wore a bathrobe in the middle of the day—her grandmother would consider him sloppy and maybe lazy—treated her as if she were a grown-up, and produced a wonderful dessert that Kate had never tasted before: blintzes, topped with sour cream and fresh cherries. Certainly not treating her like an intruder.

"You have read *War and Peace*, Miss Kate?" Sunbeams streaming through dusty blinds landed on, then bounced off, his gold tooth.

"No, Mr. Provakov, I haven't."

He turned off the radio, just after Kate had caught what sounded like the words, "Julius Rosenberg," spoken in heavily accented English, smack in the middle of a Russian sentence.

"We start today. Sophie, please bring us Tolstoy's masterpiece, and read aloud to us." Mr. Provakov hoisted his glass as if toasting Kate. "Then we discuss."

By the time they finished off the blintzes, Natasha had *almost* replaced Scarlett as her all-time favorite character in a book. And when Sophie's father said. "Good day, Katya. We read chapter two next visit," Kate had *almost* forgotten she'd heard Julius Rosenberg's name broadcast over Mr. Provakov's shortwave radio.

Eleven

The Present

"I'm waiting, Mrs. Kennedy." Detective Parker tapped a yellow pencil's eraser on his desk.

Should she bluff? How much did the detective know? Kate still wasn't sure what she knew herself. Or if her unwelcome memories from more than fifty-five years ago could be connected to Uncle Weatherwise's murder.

The phone on Parker's desk rang, a shrill ring, jarring Kate, making her jump.

"Parker." He sounded angry.

Kate felt sorry for the caller who'd interrupted the detective's interrogation.

As Parker growled, "Yes," a frightened Kate tried to plot her next move.

Parker listened for a full minute, then said, "I'll check that out, then see you later." He stood and pointed his right index finger at Kate. "Go, home, Mrs. Kennedy. I'll drop by your condo tonight."

Kate spotted a wan Marlene pacing the waiting room. Her sister-in-law managed a weak smile. "Come on, Kate, let's use our get-out-of-jail-free cards and head back east where we belong." Marlene's spunky attitude had disappeared, along with her good humor. Kate more than empathized.

They drove east toward Ocean Vista in silence, the old Chevy's top down, the sun on their faces, and the last of the hurricane's wind now only a cool breeze.

Kate sat and stewed, afraid she'd be found out, not sure how her behavior during that long-ago summer could be connected to the weatherman's murder, but afraid it was.

And what about Marlene? Quiet didn't become her.

As if reading Kate's mind—that happened a lot—Marlene broke the silence. "Kate, I think that cop and the judge kept me in court so long on purpose, you know, treating me like a felon, so I couldn't be with you. I'd bet Detective Parker set the whole thing up to be sure you'd be alone when he grilled you."

"How could Parker know you'd run a red light?" Kate asked, wondering if Marlene could be right.

"Believe me, that traffic cop had his orders. He'd have found some reason to detain me."

"Well, as it turned out, I didn't get grilled. Parker answered his phone and, though he sounded annoyed, whoever called took precedence. I was summarily dismissed. He said he'd drop by tonight."

"That's strange," Marlene said.

"Strange?"

"Why would Parker have taken a phone call when he was so hot on questioning you? He must have caller ID or else he'd left instructions with the desk officer to put someone through. Someone important. Another suspect?"

"Another? You believe I'm a suspect?"

Marlene laughed. "Not me, but Parker does. I just don't understand why."

Kate understood too well. Parker knew something about her past—or thought he did. What she'd done all those decades ago was hard to explain, even to herself. The guilt may have ebbed, but it never quite receded. Could Weatherwise have been . . .

"Kate, where are you? Lost in some daydream?" Marlene sounded impatient. "I asked you a question."

"Sorry, tell me again." More like a nightmare.

Debris, waiting to be picked up, cluttered both sides of I-95. An abandoned car abutted the highest pile.

"Should we call Mary Frances? Fill her in about the hurricane?" Marlene jerked her head toward the abandoned car. "Let her know Ocean Vista weathered the storm, that her dolls survived?"

"We can't call. She's on retreat in a cloistered convent. No phone calls. We can write."

"E-mail?"

"No, a letter. The nuns—a really strict order of Carmelites—don't have a computer. I'll write to her this afternoon."

"Well, I bet they have no TV either." Marlene shook her head. "Maybe Mary Frances doesn't even know we had a hurricane."

"Reverend Mother would read the morning newspaper and give the community a summary report after prayers. Mary Frances might be worried about her collection and her condo. I'll use FedEx."

"It's all so crazy. Why would Mary Frances Costello, Broward County's reigning tango champion and the designated sexpot of Ocean Vista," Marlene's voice took on an edge, "go off on a spiritual quest to discover whether or not she should lose her virginity? It's a no-brainer. Despite that red hair and great figure, the woman's over sixty. If not now, when?"

"Well, she *is* a former nun, Marlene. That's why she's back in Wisconsin; she's having an identity crisis. Mary Frances may be sixty, but in her heart, her soul, she's still sixteen."

"Show me a sixteen-year-old virgin and I'll spend a month in contemplation, myself." Marlene giggled. "But not in a computerless convent in Wisconsin. How would I get on Lastromance.com?"

Kate laughed, too, glad that Marlene had snapped out of her funk. Now if she could just snap out of hers.

An hour later, Kate and Marlene were walking on the beach with Ballou, amazed at how much of the cleanup had been completed.

Though Kate held the leash, the Westie led them. Today's destination, north toward the Neptune Boulevard pier.

"Ladies, please wait up a moment." Bob Seeley's voice sounded even more querulous than usual.

Kate spun around, as Ballou kept moving forward, almost losing her foothold in the sand. "Sit, Ballou." Fat chance.

The frail man appeared nervous. "Marlene, as Ocean Vista's chair of finance, I need to report some important information to our president."

Kate swallowed a giggle. Poor Bob. Such deference. You'd think Marlene was president of the United States.

"Yes, Bob, please give your report," Marlene said, sounding as if she were.

"A bid has been made on Walt Weatherwise's apartment. The offer comes from S. J. Corbin. And not for a client. Ms. Corbin wishes to reside here herself. Or so she says. Rather odd, since she already has a mansion on the Intercoastal."

Ballou struggled; Kate stumbled, but held firm. The light wind scattered sand on her terry cloth cover-up.

Marlene smiled. "Great. S. J. Corbin's the biggest Realtor in Broward County. Maybe she wants a pied a terre on the ocean. Whatever. Ocean Vista's hot. The body isn't even cold, and the most successful woman in the county wants to buy Walt's condo."

"That's the problem, Marlene." Bob sounded grave. "The offer arrived early this morning before the news of Uncle Weatherwise's death went public. Before S. J. Corbin or anyone else, except for Kate and the police, could have known there was a body."

TWELVE

"The killer knew," Kate said, spearing a coconut shrimp. "Maybe after murdering Weatherwise, he or she called S. J. Corbin. For God's sake, Bob made it sound as if I called her. As if I might have pierced Uncle Weatherwise's heart." She stabbed a second shrimp.

"Nah. Bob doesn't believe that." Marlene poured more melted butter on her lobster tail. "Who knows? Could the killer have been on commission, working for Corbin's firm, and decided to phone in a hot lead?" She adjusted her bib, just in time to blot the dripping butter. "Or could S. J. Corbin be the killer?"

Kate sniffed. "Or could Bob Seeley want you and our other neighbors to question my behavior in order to cast suspicion away from himself?"

"I know you overheard him threaten Walt, but come on, Kate. Can you picture prissy old Bob plunging a weather vane into another old blowhard's heart?"

Their favorite local haunt, the Neptune Inn, hadn't opened today, the staff still mopping up. Kate and Marlene had gone south to Sea Watch, more upscale and much dryer.

They'd both ordered cosmopolitans, served in art deco glasses. The seafood was, as Marlene had promised, to die for. And they had a beautiful view of the twilight over the ocean. Kate should have felt mellow; instead, she felt belligerent.

"Money might be the motive. I've never seen Bob like that before." Kate replayed the conversation she'd overheard in the school gym. "Desperate. In a rage. And Weatherwise threatened Bob."

"Bob appears too well bred to kill a roach. Still, he did try to sell us that cockamamie story about Rosie's tote bag." Marlene hailed a waiter, "Another round, please."

"Not for me," Kate protested. "Detective Parker is supposed to drop by tonight, though he hasn't called yet." She fingered her cell phone at the ready next to her bread plate.

"If you don't drink yours, I will." Marlene waved the waiter away.

"Then I'm driving." Less than a mile to Ocean Villa, but Kate wouldn't chance it, not with Marlene at the wheel after having downed three cocktails the size of Cleveland.

"Okay," Marlene said, then finished her first round. "What about Lucy Diamond? You gotta like a federal prosecutor for the killer. Unlike bland Bob, that broad has the temperament to stab a man in the back or in the heart. But does she have a motive?"

Kate nodded. "I'm wondering if she and Walt knew each other before Ocean Vista. Maybe in Miami? She called him an old fraud at the shelter. Sounded as though they had a history. Could Lucy have prosecuted—or attempted to prosecute—Uncle Weatherwise?"

"I'll check out Lucy's career on the computer tomorrow morning." Marlene appeared pleased with herself. "Don't worry, Miss Marple, Della Street is on the case."

"Talk about mixing mystery genres." Kate smiled, feeling less tense. Less alone. "Thanks, Marlene." How many times had she said that to her best friend over the years? Countless. A rush of gratitude enveloped her. Her *forever* friend had come through again.

"Speaking of mixing, what the hell is taking the bartender so long with our drinks?"

A slightly tipsy Marlene had handed over her car keys without a quibble. Kate navigated the big Chevy into its assigned spot in covered parking without scratching Rosie's Lincoln Continental.

At seven-thirty they walked across the pool area and through the back door into the lobby. Miss Mitford, never off duty, stood at her station, talking to an attractive brunette.

Marlene poked Kate between her shoulder blades and whispered, "That's S. J. Corbin."

"How do you know?"

"Her picture's in *Gold Coast* magazine all the time. Her real estate company runs a full-page ad in every issue." Marlene slurred the sentence, especially, the word *issue*, but that didn't stop her. "Corbin's face always fills half the space."

"Let's go say hello to our new neighbor." She spoke before thinking. Marlene could be outrageous sober; with three cosmos under her belt, God only knew what she might say. Kate didn't care; curiosity outranked concern. She had too many questions.

Marlene burped, then made a beeline to the front desk.

Miss Mitford raised a disapproving eyebrow as Kate approached.

"Good evening." Kate's smile encompassed both Mitford and Corbin. She pivoted and extended her right hand to S. J. Corbin, gesturing toward Marlene with her left. "I'm Kate Kennedy and this is my sister-in-law, Marlene Freidman. Welcome to Ocean Vista."

The Realtor flashed a set of teeth so white they dazzled. Kate must start using the bleaching kit and plastic apparatus that the dentist, at Marlene's insistence, had custom-made for her. The tray and the bleaching gel had cost almost four hundred dollars and now sat, unopened, gathering dust, in her medicine cabinet. However, Marlene's bleach job, bright as it was, couldn't compare to Corbin's movie-star smile.

"I'm delighted to meet you both. I'm going to love it here. I've always wanted to live smack on a Florida beach." S.J. spoke fast, like a New Yorker. Not with Lucy Diamond's hard *g* on the end of *going*, so often a dead giveaway of Long Island or Brooklyn roots, and not with nasal vowels, that residue from Rosie O'Grady's Bronx childhood, but more like Kate's own accent. The *a* in *Florida* sounding like *er*.

"Marlene and I love it." Kate tried to match the new owner's enthusiasm.

S.J. smiled, oozing warmth. A true sales personality. "At first, I'll only be at Ocean Vista part-time. But I'm planning on retiring, selling the big house. Not getting any younger, you know."

"That's for damn sure, S.J.," Marlene said, bowing. "Welcome to the old folks' home."

Kate, lost in thought, didn't bother to intercede.

Some Fort Lauderdale wag had once dubbed Broward County a bedroom community of New York City. Interesting how many of Ocean Vista's residents, including Kate, Marlene, and Rosie, had migrated south from the Big Apple. And, as Rosie often pointed out, Lucy Diamond and Bob Seeley had grown up "on the ass end of Long Island."

Coincidence? Kate thought not. Again, visions of the old Park Sheraton danced in her head. She took a deep breath, then plunged. "Ms. Corbin, I'm curious. How did you know that Walt Weatherwise's apartment was available?" No mincing words. Just the facts, Ma'am.

Kate hoped her query might startle the Realtor.

No such luck. Corbin, unfazed, said, "Kate, please call me, S.J., all my friends do."

"Yeah, yeah. So how about answering your new friend Kate's question?" Marlene listed to the left. Kate could smell the booze, feeling certain that S.J. and Miss Miford could, too.

"Walt told me." S.J. held her palms straight up, not unlike a magician proving he had no tricks up his sleeve.

Kate started, but spoke before Marlene, who had her mouth open, could. "Walt told you? Now I'm really confused, S.J. When you made the bid on the condo, Weatherwise was already dead, but his murder hadn't been reported anywhere."

"I had no idea Walt was dead. How could I have known?" S.J. sounded sincere, but then she sold real estate for a living. "I did know he would be moving. Nevada? Arizona? Somewhere in the desert. He'd listed his condo with me yesterday afternoon. Before the hurricane hit. His asking price seemed very low. I had the impression Walt must be in a hurry to sell, to move. He said his attorney would act as his agent, handle all the details. This morning I decided I wanted the apartment for myself, and I made my bid. Weatherwise's attorney accepted it."

"Really?" Marlene sounded doubtful, but Kate figured the Realtor must have documentation to back up her story. "Were you and Weatherwise friends?"

"Let's say Walt and I traveled in the same social set." S.J. kept smiling. "Miss Mitford tells me the police are conducting a through search of the condo, so, though I'm dying to start renovating, I have to hold off."

"Murder can be *bloody* inconvenient," Marlene said.

Ignoring Marlene, S.J. turned to Kate. "I can't wait to live here, Kate. I think we're going to be great friends."

Thirteen

Tuesday, July 4, 1950

"I think we're going to be great friends," Sophie had said as they parted the previous afternoon.

Her words lingered in this morning's memory.

"I don't want to go to Rockaway, Mom." Kate grabbed the jar of peanut butter and slammed the refrigerator door. "Can't I stay home with Etta?"

"Your grandmother is coming with us, Kate. It's the Fourth of July. Families celebrate together." Maggie Norton sighed. "And don't you dare bang that door again. Do you have any idea how much money your father spent on my present? It's a Westinghouse, Kate."

As if Kate could forget the brand name. She'd only heard it two thousand times since Christmas.

The iceman used to deliver once a week. Messy business, but kind of fun. Her mother and grandmother often slipped, referring to the fancy new refrigerator as an ice-box.

"Kate, pay attention." Her mother sounded annoyed. "You need to treat everything in this house with respect. Even appliances."

"Okay, I'll try." Kate meant it. She'd always been a compulsively neat but careless girl, breaking glasses, dropping dishes. "But, listen, Mom, I can stay here alone. I'm thirteen. You let me babysit the Martin's kids; why won't you let me spend a holiday by myself?"

Kate put two slices of toasted Wonder bread on a blue china plate and covered them both with peanut butter and strawberry jam.

"And why can't you use the everyday dishes?" Her mother was filling a gallon-size Thermos with grape juice.

"Because I like nice things, because food tastes better served on a china plate, and because the way you hoard the Wedgwood, we'll all wear out before it does."

"Watch your mouth, Katharine Norton." The full name treatment.

Kate had gone too far. She might as well change into her suit right after breakfast. Squeezing her Lipton tea bag hard against the china cup, she knew she'd be spending the day on the beach.

Etta entered the kitchen, her silver bob covered with a wide-brim, navy blue beach hat that matched her old-fashioned, skirted bathing suit. She was buttoning up an ankle-length terry cloth robe. "I'm ready. Should I start on the sandwiches? Egg salad?"

"Yes, please." Kate's mother smiled. If she resented her mother-in-law living with them, Maggie Norton had never shown it.

Kate felt good about them getting along. Marlene's

mother was always fighting with her mother-in-law, who lived in Rego Park and only visited on Sundays. Such scenes. Poor Mr. Friedman, caught in the middle.

"Are you sure you don't want to invite Marlene?" Her grandmother ventured where Kate and her mother hadn't gone. For seven summers, every Saturday and most Sundays, Marlene had driven down to Rockaway with the Norton family. Why would Etta even suggest such a thing? Where was her sense of loyalty? Kate had cried in her grandmother's arms after Marlene's betrayal.

"I will never speak to Marlene again." Kate dropped her tea cup into the saucer. She wished she could invite Sophie. Would her father find her new friend too weird? What would Sophie think about Kate's boring family?

"You're lucky that cup didn't break." Her mother sounded sad rather than angry.

"Sorry, Mom." Kate wiped up the spilled tea with her napkin.

"Look, Kate," her mother said, "you can't stay here alone. You father would have a fit. Would you like to ask someone else? Another friend? Maybe the girl you met yesterday at Miss Ida's."

Kate couldn't believe it. Had her mother read her mind? Sometimes Maggie Norton amazed her. Of course, Kate had talked a lot about Sophie over dinner last night.

"Can I call her now?"

An hour later, Sophie climbed into the black Buick's backseat with Kate and Etta.

As they drove along Woodhaven Boulevard, Kate felt grateful that her father wasn't asking Sophie a lot of dopey questions. Instead, Mom and Sophie were discussing *Kon-*

Tiki. Both were reading it; Sophie was further along. Etta chimed in about how much she liked Miss Ida, but didn't get too far. Mom and Sophie's book-review club lasted all the way to Belle Harbor. Kate, getting a little jealous, was about to change the subject when her father beat her to it.

"What does your father do, Sophie?"

"Do? I don't understand, Mr. Norton."

"For a living." Kate's father spoke slowly, enunciating every word. "You know, what's his line of work?"

Kate cringed.

"My mother goes to work. She's a secretary." Sophie also enunciated, as if crafting her response. "My father stays home."

Please God, make my father shut up. I'll go to Mass every day for a month. I'll never drink tea in a Wedgwood cup again. Just make him shut up.

Miraculously, he did. Kate would be getting up for nine o'clock Mass for the next thirty days, but her father's silence would be worth every hour of lost sleep.

Still . . . Kate wondered why Sophie hadn't mentioned her father's graphs and charts. Boris Provakov had been *working* on something yesterday. They'd interrupted him.

Twenty minutes later they were on Rockaway Beach, where Queens met the Atlantic Ocean.

Her grandmother didn't like the sun, but her parents and Kate loved it, basking in its rays from Memorial Day to Labor Day.

Hopping in the hot sand, they spread out their blankets and set up their beach chairs at just the right angle. Kate and her parents would be rotating their positions every fifteen minutes to follow the sun.

No matter how hard she tried, Kate never tanned. Too

fair skinned like her father. While her Mom took on a golden brown, Coppertone glow, Kate and her dad just got redder and redder. But she loved how the sun turned the hairs on her arms to gold and streaked her chestnut brown curls with blonde highlights.

Etta sank into a folding chair, facing the boardwalk; she'd spend the day shifting away from direct sunlight.

Kate's father had brought his homemade brew of Lipton tea, Lanolin, and baby oil. He'd been using the smelly mix for years and, though the tea stained his skin to a red-bronze, he never tanned, either.

Sophie wearing an old-fashioned, navy wool bathing suit, had dynamite color. "Tar Beach," she answered when Kate's mother asked where she'd gotten her beautiful tan.

Kate's parents and Etta laughed at Sophie's response. Kate didn't get the joke. "Where's Tar Beach?"

Her father laughed again. "On the roof, Katie. When we lived on the West Side, we went to Tar Beach all the time. Swam in the Hudson River, too."

Never having lived in an apartment house or a tenement, Kate felt deprived. The only one never to have experienced Tar Beach.

While her mother set up housekeeping—Maggie Norton liked order, even in the sand—Kate and Sophie walked to the water's edge.

A good-looking young lifeguard waved at them. Well, at Sophie. In her two-piece yellow gingham bathing suit, Kate looked flat-chested. Looked like a child.

The jetty to their left was covered with seaweed, the waves breaking at their feet, the smell of salt tingling her nose. All her favorite memories from summers past. Kate should be happy, but something felt wrong.

•　•　•

Kate ran into the ocean, not even reacting to the cold jolt that swept over her body.

Sophie dove into a huge wave, popped back up, and, using a strong Esther Williams–style breaststoke, swam into the deep water.

"Hey," Kate yelled, "my mother doesn't want us in over our heads."

Not to mention that Kate felt terror when she couldn't touch bottom.

"Okay, let's swim sideways, away from the jetty."

"Great backstroke," Sophie said. And Kate couldn't believe how much her mood improved.

Sitting in the damp sand, watching the boys watching the girls, Kate said, "My father works for Sinclair Oil in a skyscraper on Fifth Avenue, near Tiffany's." She hadn't planned to say any of that; the words just tumbled out. "Some job in management. His address is 666. Dad says it's the sign of the devil."

"Yes, it's in the Bible." Sophie laughed. "My father would consider the address appropriate for an oil company."

Figuring in for a dime, in for a dollar, Kate asked, "What does your father do with all those charts and graphs?"

Sophie frowned. "I've never asked Poppa what he does."

"And he doesn't talk about it?" Kate found that hard to believe. "My father bores us to death at dinner, rambling on and on about Sinclair."

"Not really." A stream of wet sand ran trough Sophie's fingers. "Whatever the project is, it's been going on forever. Something to do with tides and winds. Something to do with the weather."

Fourteen

The Present

An exhausted Kate, dying to get out of her clothes and into her version of pajamas—one of Charlie's oversized T-shirts and sweatpants—paced. Where the devil was Detective Parker?

The clock in the front hall—her late husband's favorite Kennedy family heirloom and one of the few treasures from Kate's beloved Tudor in Rockville Centre—chimed nine.

Damn Parker. She added *discourteous* to the detective's growing list of negatives.

If Miss Miford had gone home—doubtful; the sentinel probably slept in some cubbyhole behind the front desk—Kate would have to buzz Parker into Ocean Vista. Unless, of course, he was interviewing another suspect first.

When had she accepted that she was a suspect?

She'd give him till ten, then pull her phone, turn off her cell, and disconnect her intercom. He could just reschedule tomorrow. Parker deserved no less.

Tomorrow. The mess in the living room nagged her. She'd finish the hurricane cleanup in the morning. Kate thrived on order. Charlie used to tease that June Cleaver and Frank Gilbreth, the efficiency expert in *Cheaper by the Dozen*, were her role models. She laughed as she headed for the kitchen to put on the kettle. "Oh, Charlie, did you ever know how right you were?"

Trying to decide between high-test or decaf Lipton, Kate jumped when someone rapped hard on the front door. Ballou, who'd retired for the night, barked. Kate shut off the whistling kettle and hurried back to the hall, the Westie at her heels. How could the detective have gotten into the building without being announced or buzzed up?

Maybe her caller wasn't Parker. She used the peephole for the first time in the fifteen months that she'd lived here. Drat. She couldn't see a bloody thing.

"Who is it?" She sounded strident.

"Lucy Diamond. Open the damn door." Lucy's voice, pitched several decibels higher than Kate's, bordered on hysteria.

Kate opened the door. Her uninvited guest, in a bright green sweatsuit, strode into the living room, Ballou sniffing at her sneakers.

Without being asked, Lucy sat—almost collapsed—on Kate's off-white couch. She looked haggard. Frightened.

"Would you like a cup of tea? Or maybe a drink?"

"Scotch. Straight up." Lucy barked, then chortled. "Thanks. Sorry, guess I'm too upset to mind my manners."

Kate located a bottle of Johnnie Walker Black on a shelf behind the wet bar in the dining room. Nary a highball or a lowball glass in sight. A testament to the changing tastes in booze over the last few decades. Only wineglasses. Hmm? Red or white?

"What's wrong, Lucy?" Kate handed her a red wineglass half filled with scotch.

"Detective Parker." Lucy coated her words with venom. "Thinks I killed Walt." She downed most of the scotch in one gulp. "Do you think so, too, Kate?"

Nothing, if not direct. Kate almost replied, You're certainly on my list, but, instead, shook her head and said nothing.

"That's why I was out there at Coral Reef Police Station this afternoon, but you knew that, didn't you?"

For a woman drinking Charlie's best scotch, Lucy Diamond behaved as if she were prosecuting Kate. And, for sure, this hadn't been Lucy's first drink of the night.

Kate, too tired to take her guest's guff, lashed out. "When we were being evacuated, did you cross the bridge next to Walt Weatherwise?"

"What the hell difference could that possibly make, Kate?" Lucy drained her scotch. "But, for your information, Walt crossed between Rosie and Bob."

Damn. Why, of all the questions she'd wanted to ask Lucy, had she started with that one? Dumb move, Kate.

"You overheard me fighting with Walt in the gym, didn't you?" Lucy held out her glass. "God knows, I wanted to kill the bastard, but I didn't. Pour me another drink and I'll tell you a story. A sad story."

Suspecting this would be a another long night, Kate poured herself a white wine.

Turning, she raised her glass. "To sad stories. I'm

listening." Kate hadn't overheard much of anything between Lucy and Walt in the gym, but if Lucy believed she had, why should Kate correct her?

Lucy nodded, quiet now. Preparing her opening statement?

Kate sank into a chenille armchair. Edmund had described the chair's color as butter pecan. If she had to compare the chair's color to ice cream, Kate thought it looked more like toasted almond.

For a fleeting moment, she could hear the ring of the bell on the Good Humor man's bicycle, feel the cold blast from the freezer box in front of his handlebars cooling her sweaty face, taste her favorite toasted almond bar, savor the last lick of ice cream off the wooden stick. Then she started, scolding herself: Focus, Kate, focus. Get the hell out of the past.

"Weatherwise and I go back a long way." Lucy's agitation had vanished. She appeared stronger, calmer. Had some of her earlier histrionics been an act? Or had her professional demeanor taken over—going on automatic pilot—as she prepared to present her case?

It was Kate's turn to nod.

"Fifteen years ago," Lucy said, "long before my hair turned white and I began dying it black, long before I retired and started collecting Social Security, long before I lost most of my muscle tone and any semblance of a positive attitude, I met Walt Weatherwise in Miami Beach at the Blue Parrot, a swinging singles bar for middle-age loners. Make that losers."

Kate sipped her wine, hoping she could nurse it through Lucy's maudlin saga.

"He not only stole my heart, he compromised my integrity. A deadly combination for a federal prosecutor's suitor."

"What happened?" Kate tried to steer Lucy away from emotion and into a few facts.

"Well, as you know, Walt wasn't much to look at, but back then the man's conquests were legion. The PR people at the TV station planted tabloid stories bragging that Weatherwise had bedded 20 percent of his female viewers. Our affair began at his oceanfront mansion in South Beach; it would have put Hugh Hefner's to shame."

Had Lucy visited the *Playboy* publisher's mansion, too? Kate decided she didn't need to know.

"Early on and totally smitten, I figured Walt lived way above his income. Yes, he had a high salary, but his lifestyle and his toys, including a yacht with gold faucets in the head, seemed far too grand, even for a television icon." Lucy paused and drained her drink. She held up her glass, seeming surprised to discover it was empty.

"Another?" Kate felt like a pusher.

"Make it one for the road," Lucy sang, then laughed as if she had Jay Leno's wit.

On her way to the bar, Kate cut to the chase. "Where did Weatherwise get all that money?"

"If I could have answered that question, I'd have prosecuted the bastard. He broke my heart, Kate."

A woman scorned. Worse, a federal prosecutor scorned.

Kate thought of Rosie O'Grady dating Albert Anastasia. Of Marlene's penchant for bad boys. Was she the only woman in Ocean Vista who'd slept on the right side of the law?

"I gave it my best," Lucy said. "Tried to get Walt for income tax evasion, for hiding assets—probably from illegal trading, maybe using another name—then transferring the cash into a foreign account, but I could never locate the source of the money or gather enough proof to indict the son of a bitch. He'd hired F. Lee Bailey. One of his last cases."

"Strange that both you and Walt wound up at Ocean Vista." And what about Bob Seeley? Kate felt sure Walt's threat to Bob last night and his demand for money had been connected to all this. Could Bob have been a partner in Weatherwise's crooked deals? Had fussy old Bob been a money launderer?

"Not strange at all. Walt had a new lady in his life. He convinced the network that he could report the weather from its Fort Lauderdale studio, and he moved from Miami to be near his lover."

"How do you know all this?"

The phone rang. Damn. Lee Parker, she presumed. Kate *had* to take the call.

"Hi," she said, motioning to Lucy to stay seated.

"Kate, it's Mary Frances. This is the first chance I've had since the hurricane to sneak a phone call. How are my dolls? Were they in harm's way? Any water damage? Are Jackie and Marilyn okay?"

"Yes, they're all fine. Marlene and I are doing okay, too."

"Well, thank God. I haven't been able to sleep. I've been so worried about my girls. And, er, about you and Marlene, and, of course, Joe."

"All is well here at Ocean Vista. Look, I can't talk, Mary Frances. I have company."

"I'm coming home, Kate. I've made a decision regarding my virginity."

A loud banging at the front door made Lucy drop her

drink. She jumped up and started toward the hall. The clock chimed.

"Pro or con, Mary Frances?" Kate asked.

Lucy opened the door.

Rosie O'Grady ran in, screaming. "Kate, come quick. There's a dead body bleeding all over the backseat of my Lincoln Continental."

Fifteen

The man lay facedown in a pool of blood. A knife stuck in his neck. Kate, kneeling on the front passenger seat, didn't want to touch or move the body. She had no need to see his face. She'd know him anywhere. Why hadn't Rosie recognized Detective Parker?

"Call the police," Kate yelled to no one, to everyone. She couldn't pull her eyes away from the dead man.

"And an ambulance," Lucy said, suddenly sober.

"Right." Kate agreed, though she felt certain it was too late to help Lee Parker.

"Whaddaya think?" Rosie said. "I watch *Law & Order*. I knocked on Marlene's door first and asked her to call the cops; then I took the elevator up to get you, Kate."

"So much blood. You wouldn't think there'd be so much blood." Lucy, trying to peer over Kate's shoulder, sounded like Lady Macbeth. She must have performed well in the courtroom.

Of course there would be a lot of blood. The killer had sliced the jugular. Parker's head listed to the left, as if his neck had been broken. Could that, too, be result of a knife wound? Somehow Kate didn't think so.

And why in the world had Parker gotten into the backseat of Rosie's car? The body hadn't been there when she and Marlene returned from the Sea Watch and parked next to the Lincoln, had it? She didn't remember looking into the car, so she couldn't be sure. And the blood looked fresh. He couldn't have been dead long.

Not wanting to leave fingerprints, Kate inched out of the front seat and through the passenger door the same way she'd crawled in, without using her hands. "It's Detective Parker."

Lucy gasped, then teetered. Had she not recognized the body either?

"Why did that cop have to get himself killed in my car?" Rosie hurled her question at Kate as if she expected Kate had the answer. "I just had the seats reupholstered, ya know. Cost me more than my entire July Social Security payment. There ain't no justice."

"Life's a bitch, Rosie," Lucy snapped, then wiped her eyes.

Strange. Parker's demise might let Lucy off the hook for Weatherwise's murder, but she was carrying on as if she'd lost the love of her life. Or was she mourning unrequited love?

Kate turned to Rosie and realized for the first time that the former Rockette was dressed to kill. In blood red. A full-skirted chiffon cocktail dress, not unlike a bridesmaid circa 1957. Matching strappy sandals, flattering those great legs, last noticed wrapped around Uncle Weatherwise's neck. And enough rhinestones, glittering like tinsel, to trim a tabletop-size Christmas tree.

"Where were you going?" Kate assumed that Rosie hadn't been driving home with a dead detective in her backseat, but still, ten P.M. was pretty late for an eighty-four-year-old to be starting out.

"Dancing." Defiant in body language and tone. "At Ireland's Inn."

Kate waited.

"I was watching my Lawrence Welk video and got nostalgic, ya know, wanted a little companionship. A little smooth dancing. In someone's arms." Rosie stared down at the ground. "Maybe an old-fashioned. My favorite cocktail." It had been Kate's father's favorite, too. "I figured I'd run into Joe Sajak at Ireland's." She jerked her thumb toward an empty spot across the parking lot. "His car wasn't there, so I was right, he'd gone dancing."

Kate had dropped the phone before hearing Mary Frances's decision. She hoped the former nun wouldn't be losing her virginity to snaky Sajak.

A Paul Newman lookalike, once a suspect in his wife's murder, Joe had most of Ocean Vista's widows and divorcees dropping off casseroles and inviting him to dinner on Las Olas and plays—that they "just happened to have an extra ticket for"—at the Broward County Performing Arts Center. The man made Kate squirm. How well had Joe known Uncle Weatherwise? And what time had he left for Ireland's Inn?

"Kate!" Marlene, her platinum hair in huge pink plastic rollers, wearing a marabou-trimmed, white satin dressing gown, had arrived, dragging an ashen Bob, in tailored—probably Brooks Brothers—pressed pajamas, behind her.

An ambulance's siren heralded its arrival and a

Palmetto Beach Police car, lights flashing, pulled into the parking lot behind it.

"The 911 operator wouldn't let me off the phone. Reporting a dead body isn't easy. Questions. Questions. Details. Details. I finally told her I'd been stabbed, too, and hung up." Marlene groaned. "So here I am, and not a second too soon."

"Let me go, Marlene." Bob looked even thinner than usual. And frightened. "You roused me out of bed, mumbling something about a murder in the parking lot." He came across as vague, his breathing labored.

Marlene gestured to the police car, literally shoved Bob at Lucy, and whispered in Kate's ear. "Around eight-thirty or so, I was sitting on my balcony having a nightcap."

A nightcap. After three cosmos at dinner. Kate sighed, then asked "And?"

The August night air surrounded them like wet woolen drapes, smothering, relentless in its stillness.

"And I watched as someone left the beach, came through the pool gate, and headed into the parking lot." Marlene had stepped back, but kept her voice low.

"Who?" Marlene's dramatic delivery, an obvious attempt to build up suspense, was annoying Kate.

"Your new best friend, S. J. Corbin. At the time I didn't think much of it, figured she'd been checking out the beach and was on her way to get her car."

"Kate Kennedy." She spun around. Nick Carbone, sweating in a wrinkled blue shirt, walked toward her. "So you've discovered two bodies in two days. Is that your personal best?"

"Hey, I found this stiff." Rosie oozed indignation. "If ya got any questions, Detective Carbone, fire away. I'm kinda in a hurry, ya know. And when can you get

Detective Parker's body out of my car? I'd like to catch
the last set at Ireland's Inn."

Carbone flushed. His olive skin turned redder than
Rosie's dress. "You're not going anywhere, Ms. O'Grady."

Kate leaned against the hood of Marlene's car, feeling
faint from the heat, but trying to focus. Pajamas popped
into her mind. Why were Bob Seeley's pajamas so crisply
pressed if, as he said, Marlene had just roused him from
bed?

sixteen

In what Kate considered very unorthodox police procedure, Nick Carbone had led them all, including Miss Mitford, who'd been hovering at the front desk, into Ocean Vista's recreation room, ordered them to sit there and wait, instructed a uniformed officer to stay behind, then returned to the scene of the crime. The sudden move from oppressive heat to aggressive air-conditioning left Kate wishing she had a sweater.

The young policeman, in his slightly wilted, but otherwise spiffy Palmetto Beach uniform, inhibited conversation. Too bad. Some of Kate's many questions might have been inadvertently answered; people said the damnedest things under stress.

Oh well, there was always body language.

Miss Mitford's crossed arms and furrowed brow shouted indignation. She sat, her back ramrod straight, far removed from the condo owners, in a chair near the door to the lobby, seemingly ready to return to sentinel duty as soon as the inquisition ended.

Lucy paced in front of a dais still covered in red, white, and blue crepe-paper streamers from the Fourth of July party. In the harsh, fluorescent lighting, the former prosecutor appeared haggard. Kate felt grateful she couldn't see herself, sure she looked like death warmed over, one of her grandmother's many right on-target descriptions.

Bob Seeley's expensive navy blue pajamas remained as stiff as his personality. Nary a wrinkle. How could that be? No sweat? Strong starch? A great, no-iron-needed miracle fabric? Still ashen, he held his hands in his lap, and stared down at his matching leather slippers. Bob didn't strike Kate as a man who'd appear in public in his nightclothes. Even if awakened by Marlene and confused about what had happened or who'd been murdered. Could his vagueness and the pajamas be props? Part of an act? Not unlike Lucy acting so sorry about Lee Parker's death.

Marlene fidgeted with the marabou, tugging her dressing gown closer, adjusting the slippery satin sash, pulling it tighter.

Rosie O'Grady broke the silence, whistling, rather well, "Shall We Dance? The young cop, standing a few feet in front of Rosie, smiled and tapped his right foot.

Kate, remembering what Charlie had told her about how the New York City DA's office advised their witnesses to behave in court, sat as straight as Miss Mitford, with uncrossed legs, feet planted on the floor, hands folded in her lap. She hoped her demeanor would impress Nick Carbone.

Within five minutes, everyone in the room was either pacing or squirming in their seats, including Kate. So much for her courtroom decorum.

She'd just started to review the timeline—who'd been where—during what appeared to be a relatively narrow window of opportunity, when Nick Carbone returned with a distraught S. J. Corbin in tow.

"I told you I was getting a tape measure from my car, for heaven's sake. You have no right to hold me, Detective Carbone." S.J.'s voice quaked.

"Please take a seat, Ms. Corbin. I'm investigating the death of a homicide detective who was working a murder case in my town."

A cop had been killed. Kate remembered how Charlie would close down, racked with sorrow, full of fury, and itching for revenge when a NYPD cop fell in the line of duty.

Carbone, sweating while Kate shivered, wiped his brow. "Not only do I have the right, I have the duty to question everyone in this room." His clipped words several degrees colder than the air-conditioning.

What would Nick say if she asked to be excused to get a sweater? She almost laughed aloud at the thought. Better to suffer in silence.

"The initial CSI report indicates that Detective Lee Parker died from unnatural causes no earlier than seven-thirty P.M. The 911 call from Ms. Friedman was received at nine-thirty-four. If Ms. O'Grady ran straight to Ms. Friedman's condo immediately after spotting the body, we know Parker was killed before nine-thirty."

"Whadda mean by *if*?" Rosie roared, jumping up from her front-row seat. "You think I stopped off at my apartment to pee or ditch the knife?"

"I don't know, Ms. O'Grady." He sounded steely. "Why don't you tell us about the events leading up to and directly following your discovery of Detective Parker's body? And please, do feel free to reveal where you hid the murder weapon."

Ouch. Had someone told Nick about the weather vane in Rosie's tote bag?

Questioning the suspects in front of each other struck Kate as surreal. If she, as so often accused by the detective, liked playing Miss Marple, Carbone had morphed into Hercule Poirot. Surprisingly, the Ocean Vista residents played along. All that was missing was the London drawing room.

"Who wants to stay alone in her room?" Rosie, the trouper, warmed to her tale. "Watching them dancers waltzing on the nine o'clock Welk rerun—you can check *TV Guide*—sent me out into the night. Luckily, I always wear full makeup, so I got myself dressed and was in the parking lot before nine-thirty."

Kate marveled. Rosie made a compelling, totally believable witness.

"I jest switched on the ignition when I spotted him. Don't know what made me turn around; maybe I caught a peek of something in the rearview mirror. " She shrugged, then clasped her arms in front of her chest. Another marvel. Her bare eighty-four-year-old arms were almost firm. "Don't know. So much blood. I never touched him. Didn't even get close. Jest jumped out of the car. I don't have a cell phone, so I ran like hell to Marlene's. While she called 911, I went up to Kate's. I didn't want to go back to the parking lot alone."

"You had no idea the man was Detective Parker?" Carbone raised a bushy right eyebrow.

"Right." Rosie said. "No idea."

"Weren't you the least bit curious about the identity of

the corpse in your backseat? And don't you lock your car, Ms. O'Grady?"

"Not curious enough to touch him. I figured he wasn't going nowhere. I could wait," Rosie rasped; it sounded like a smothered laugh. "And, Detective, in case you haven't noticed, I'm an old lady; maybe I forgot to lock my car. Sue me." She hiked up her bloodred dress's bodice to cover an exposed bit of black lace on her bra.

Score one for the former Radio City Rockette. She'd kicked Nick Carbone's questions off center stage and into the rear balcony.

In some perverse way, Kate was enjoying herself. She felt a pang of shame, but no remorse. Who'd be next?

seventeen

"Mrs. Kennedy, where were you between seven and nine?"

Her stomach lurched. Served her right, thriving on other people's discomfort, rooting for a suspect instead of law and order. Nick usually called her Kate. But she had no reason to be nervous. She could account for every moment, couldn't she?

"Well." Her voice seemed scratchy, prissy. "Marlene and I had dinner at the Sea Watch. We got home at seven-thirty. I remember checking my watch as we crossed the pool area. Then, in the lobby, Miss Mitford introduced us to S. J. Corbin, who's buying Walt Weatherwise's condo."

"Ms. Freidman's assigned parking spot is right next to Ms. O'Grady's, isn't it?" Carbone asked, though he knew the answer. "And her Lincoln Continental was there when you parked, right?"

"Yes." Kate said. Less nasal. Maybe a little more confident.

"Did either of you ladies notice anything different about Ms. O'Grady's car?"

Kate shook her head. "We had no reason to check it out."

"What happened after you left the lobby?"

"I went to my apartment; Marlene went to hers." Kate hesitated. "I'd expected Detective Parker, but he never called. Never showed up."

"You had another visitor, didn't you?"

"Yes, Lucy Diamond."

"And what did Ms. Diamond want?" Nick pulled out a notebook. Her answers were going on record.

What could Kate say? That Lucy dropped by to confess Detective Parker thought she'd stabbed Uncle Weatherwise. Kate stalled, trying to come up with some semblance of the truth. Though she willed herself not to, Kate's eyes sought out Lucy's. Panic filled those dark brown eyes. Lucy's jaw sagged and her shoulders had slumped. Kate forced herself to face Nick Carbone, to smile. "Girl talk."

"Girl talk?" Carbone chuckled. A condescending chuckle.

"Right." Kate was firm. "Before we really got started, Rosie O'Grady banged on my door."

Lucy sighed. In the silent room, her deep breath heaved, then lingered in the dead air. Jeez, did she think Carbone was deaf? What sort of prosecutor had this woman been? The detective raised a brow, but gave the sigh a pass.

"Why was Detective Parker coming to see you, Mrs. Kennedy?"

"His interview with me at the Coral Reef Police Headquarters was interrupted by a phone call. He excused himself to take the call, saying he'd see me tonight. Here, in Ocean Vista."

"That call was most suspicious," Marlene broke in. "Either the killer or a tipster must have been on the phone. Someone—or something—very important and urgent enough to make Parker stop interrogating his prime suspect."

Good God. With friends like Marlene, Kate could wind up in jail.

Carbone almost grinned, then ignored Marlene and moved on to Lucy. "According to Miss Mitford, Ocean Vista's officers have the four spots closest to the condo's rear entrance. Ms. Friedman's and Ms. O'Grady's to the south. Bob Seeley's and yours to the north, nearest the back door. Is that right, Ms. Diamond?"

"Correct." Lucy, standing tall and lean, met Nick's gaze. Her reply crisp, her posture straight. Her attitude a total metamorphosis.

"Where were you between seven-thirty and nine, Ms. Diamond?"

"I object to both your question and your tone, Detective." The lawyer in Lucy had surfaced. "However, in the interest of moving this investigation along, I will answer it." Lucy gestured toward a pale Bob. "Mr. Seeley and I dined at the Olympia Diner on Commercial Boulevard. We left here a little before seven and returned about eight-fifteen or so. If I'd known there had been a murder, I'd have checked my watch."

"Did you drive to the diner in your car?"

"Yes."

"Did you see Ms. Friedman's car when you left?"

"No. Marlene's parking space was empty."

"What about Ms. O'Grady's Lincoln?"

Lucy nodded. "Rosie's car was there."

"Did you notice anything unusual about it?"

With a shake of her head, Lucy said, "No. I didn't peek in the window, Detective."

"How about you, Mr. Seeley?" Nick Carbone spun in Bob's direction, obviously catching the older man by surprise. "Notice anything odd? Out of place?"

"Nothing at all, Detective."

"What did you do when you returned home after dinner?"

"I changed into my pajamas and got into bed. I'm reading the new Michael Connelly, but after a few pages, I fell asleep."

A very sedate sleeper or a very smooth liar.

"Early to bed, hey?" Carbone smiled. "Then what?"

"Marlene banging on the door and screaming bloody murder woke me up." Bob crossed his arms. "Still half asleep, I followed her out to the parking lot."

Carbone jotted something in his notebook. Kate, curious, wondered if the detective believed Bob. She found his alibi the weakest.

S. J. Corbin fiddled with a piece of torn fabric on her chair, watching and waiting. She had to know she'd be next. Would Carbone discover that S.J. had gone through the pool and into the parking lot during that brief window of opportunity he'd described? Or could he already be aware of that? Kate glanced over at the prim sentinel who sat posture perfect, serene, and confident. Maybe Miss Mitford had informed him.

"When did you arrive, Ms. Corbin?" Nick's tone softened. Why?

"About seven-fifteen. A few minutes later, Miss Mitford introduced me to my new neighbors, Kate and Marlene."

Humph. New neighbors. First names. A bit premature. Corbin's contract wasn't even signed yet. Or was it?

"Then what?" Carbone scribbled in his notebook.

"I went up to Walt Weatherwise's—er, I guess it's now my apartment."

"You had a key?"

"I'm the Realtor as well as the buyer, Detective. Mr. Weatherwise left the key at the front desk for me. I wanted to do a walk-through. Take some measurements. Check out the view at night."

"But you explored more than the apartment, didn't you?"

"Why, yes, I did." S.J. showed no surprise at his question. "I'd forgotten my tape measure, left it in the car. When I went out the back door, the moon looked so inviting that I decided to take a walk on the beach before heading to the parking lot to get my tape."

"What time did you hit the beach, Ms. Corbin?"

"Around eight-thirty, I guess."

"A long walk-through."

S. J. Corbin nodded. "Yes, I jotted down lots of information, Detective Carbone." She pointed to his notebook. "Just like you are now."

"Have you taken karate lessons, Ms. Corbin?"

Out of left field. Where in the world was Carbone going?

"No." S.J. sounded genuinely puzzled. "Why do you ask?"

"It seems a blow to the neck rendered Detective Parker unconscious before he was stabbed."

As if choreographed, Lucy, Bob, Marlene, and Kate swung their heads around to confront Rosie, who held a black belt in karate.

Eighteen

"Last night I dreamt I went to Miami again," Marlene said, bounding through Kate's front door.

Her sister-in-law's opening line evoked *Rebecca*'s, not to mention memories of Marlene's last jaunt to Miami when she'd stolen her date's wallet and his car. All for the greater good, of course.

Marlene petted a delighted Ballou, so excited to see his favorite aunt he literally jumped for joy, then she followed Kate to the kitchen and plopped a bag of still-warm bagels on the table. The smell tantalized.

"You've been to Einstein's already. I'm impressed." Kate rubbed sleep from her eyes.

"I've been up since seven," Marlene, the nocturnal, said with pride. "The early-bird detective catches the killer."

Kate groaned.

"Listen, my dream about Miami got me thinking."

"Strawberry cream cheese, too." Kate rummaged through the bag. "This is a treat."

"Look in the other bag. Tea with a splash of milk for you. A double latte for me. Eat up and get dressed. We're going to Miami."

"Why?" Kate smeared cream cheese on both sides of her plain, untoasted bagel. Just the way she liked it. Marlene could be very thoughtful when she wasn't being a pain in the tush. "I'm really tired. How come you're so peppy this morning?"

Marlene, who watched old movies on cable until the wee hours of the morning when not out on the town, preferred to rise around eleven. Ten A.M. required a wake-up call.

"Last night," Marlene spoke around a bite of bagel, "as Lucy and Bob were suffering through Carbone's inquisition, I had Miami on my mind. They both lived there at the same time that Weatherwise did, you know. And I remembered our new neighbor, S. J. Corbin, has a branch office in Miami Beach. Then I had this strange dream, so, naturally, we have to go."

Kate savored her tea while waiting for Marlene's rambling to turn into simple declarative sentences. Why did everything taste better when someone else had brewed it, baked it, or even just boiled it? She giggled. Obviously, her thoughts rambled, too.

"Don't laugh, Kate. I'm convinced that the motive's in Miami." Marlene slipped Ballou a bit of bagel.

"That must have been quite a dream." Kate hoped she sounded sincere. Marlene seemed so deadly serious that Kate didn't even scold her for feeding the Westie at the table.

"Charlie, you, and I were all in Miami, sitting in the

lobby of the Casablanca. The hotel looked exactly the same as when we'd vacationed there in 1962. Remember the over-the-top faux Moroccan decor? And Kevin appeared in the dream, too."

Marlene was referring to Charlie's brother Kevin, her divorced, and now deceased, second husband, not to Kate and Charlie's son Kevin, who'd been named for his uncle. Marlene and Kevin had been married in 1962 when the two couples had gone to Miami.

"Anyway, in my dream, Charlie said that the killer had decided to eliminate Weatherwise ages ago."

Kate felt an irrational pang of jealousy. Why was Charlie showing up in Marlene's dreams?

"Since none of them have lived here very long, that would lead us back to Miami, right?" Marlene reached for another bagel.

"What did Kevin have to say? Or didn't your former husband want to talk to you?"

Marlene flushed, then fidgeted with her coffee cup, avoiding eye contact.

Kate wished she could sallow her words. "Sorry. I guess I felt left out." She hesitated. "Jealous." She almost choked on the word, but she'd hurt Marlene; it had to be spoken. "Charlie hasn't haunted my dreams for months."

"Oh God, Kate, I'm sorry. I shouldn't have rattled on like that." Marlene's face had turned scarlet and her breathing seemed labored. "I never want to hurt you again."

"I'm sorry, too." Kate patted Marlene's hand. "No one's responsible for their dreams or who shows up in them. Let's put this behind us. Even though I should stay here and clean up from Harriet, I'll go to Miami with you.

Who knows? We might discover who killed Uncle Weatherwise."

Marlene smiled, wiped her face, and took a deep breath. "Good." She pushed her plate away, the second bagel untouched. Kate couldn't recall Marlene ever having left a bagel behind. "I'm going home to change. I can't poke around South Beach wearing these baggy old capris."

As she stacked the dishes in the sink, Kate wondered exactly what Marlene had meant by *again* when she'd said, "I never want to hurt you again."

Nineteen

Driving south on A1A with the top down, they swapped information and planned their itinerary. Only intermittent debris, piled in neat stacks on the sand, gave any hint of Tuesday's hurricane. Today, with the sky as blue as Paul Newman's eyes, the aqua water calm, the light breeze belying the heat and humidity, and the tropical setting so serene, Harriet seemed like ancient history.

"I Googled Bob and Lucy." Marlene said. "Turns out he was Southern Trust's hottest financial planner for Miami's A-list millionaires. Maybe Walt was one of Bob's clients. And you know Lucy spent years trying to send Weatherwise to jail. As condo prez, I have access to all the owners' files. I printed out Lucy's and Bob's former addresses. Weatherwise's place in South Beach and S. J. Corbin's real estate company, too. I suggest we start with Walt's mansion. Chat up his rich neighbors." Marlene pointed to a map on the dashboard in front of Kate. "His mansion's only a few blocks north of the real estate office."

"Pretty pricey area," Kate said, adjusting her prescription sunglasses, then glancing at the map. "Corbin must be really successful."

"I'd say so. And Weatherwise's house is right next to Versace's. I wonder if Donatella will invite us in, offer us a glass of white wine."

Kate giggled, picturing the elegant Donatella Versace, an international fashion designer and business mogul, asking two *mature* ladies from Palmetto Beach in for drinks.

Why did some old people sound and act so much older than others? Kate felt a surge of gratitude that she and Marlene still giggled like teenagers.

"I think she sold the place, Marlene."

"Damn."

Kate looked up from the map, letting the sun warm her face, basking in its rays. She'd applied a ton of sunblock, so maybe just a tinge of color wouldn't hurt. She could easily doze off, but had to stay awake and keep the driver company.

The driver was singing show tunes, off-key.

When A1A veered inland, Kate interrupted Marlene's rendition of "Look at Me, I'm Sandra Dee." "Mary Frances called last night, worried about her dolls. In all the excitement, I forgot to tell you."

"Is she coming home?"

"Rosie banged at my door, screaming about a bloody body, so I had to hang up, but yes, Mary Frances said she's coming home and has decided to give up her virginity."

"Even the dancing ex-nun deserves better than Joe Sajak."

"You don't think he could have killed Weatherwise and Parker, do you?" Kate sounded hopeful.

"Negative on Parker's murder. Joe left Ocean Vista before six-thirty yesterday evening. I ran into him in the lobby while I was waiting for you. Said he was driving up to Stuart to visit a lady friend for a few days."

"So he's in the clear. Too bad. Mary Frances would never have had sex with a murder suspect."

A few miles south, they were driving alongside the ocean again. Marlene had stopped singing and appeared deep in thought. Knowing her sister-in-law seldom kept even a fleeting thought to herself, Kate waited.

Not wanting to press her luck and feeling hot and flushed, she'd pulled the brim of her hat down over her face and applied more sunblock. Marlene's tan, on the other hand, grew darker as they drove.

"Kate, we're on the proverbial wild goose chase, but unless we find some evidence to the contrary, Carbone's going to arrest Rosie."

"You think she did it?"

"Well, according to Bob, she had a weather vane in her tote bag at the gym, and she's the only certified karate killer in Ocean Vista."

Kate shook her head. "A black belt isn't a license to kill."

"For God's sake, Kate, the backseat of her Lincoln was the crime scene."

"If the door was unlocked, someone else could have lured Lee Parker into Rosie's car."

"Really?" Marlene's voice dripped doubt. "And just how would *someone else* have known the Lincoln would be unlocked?"

Kate hated it when Marlene's thinking proved more

logical than her own. "You have a point." She sighed. "But I'll bet someone did. I just can't picture Rosie as a double murderer."

"Is old pisspot Bob a better candidate? Maybe. If he was Weatherwise's financial planner, he might have hidden those funds that Lucy couldn't track. Or is Lucy our killer? A frustrated former federal prosecutor and a woman scorned. I'm rooting for S. J. Corbin. We need to check out her past. I don't like her and I don't trust her. And I'd bet those feelings are mutual."

"Unlike the others, S.J. doesn't appear to have a motive." Kate shook her head. "Still . . . her trip to the parking lot certainly provided her with the opportunity."

"Maybe she had the knife in her car along with the tape measure." Marlene jutted her chin toward the west. "Enough about S. J. Corbin. Look right, Kate. The city of Miami awaits us."

Miami boasted an impressive skyline. Very tall, very modern office buildings dominated, but traditional church steeples and the old tower clock added contrast and charm. And Kate loved the juxtaposition of the ocean to the left and the sea of glass buildings—many of them tinted green—to the right.

They drove south on Collins Boulevard. Uncle Weatherwise's gated, beachfront mansion was in walking distance of several popular nightclubs, upscale sidewalk cafes, and refurbished art deco hotels.

Less than fifteen years ago, the hotels had been run-down and filled with retirees. As South Beach and its real estate grew trendier and more expensive, the old folks who'd lived there for decades were forced to move west or north or, maybe, to the cemetery.

Now nubile girls with bare midriffs and well-toned boys, prettier than the girls, skated on the sidewalk.

They valet parked at an Indian restaurant, three blocks from the mansion. It would cost plenty, and they'd have to eat lunch there, also a small fortune, but there wasn't any other option.

"We're walking by some of the most expensive property in Florida," Marlene said.

In America, Kate thought.

The gate to the pink stucco mansion wasn't locked. Beds of hibiscus in the same shade of pink lined the driveway to a back door, framed with stained-glass windows. The front entrance would open onto the sand.

Wondering if Weatherwise had sold the mansion and a new owner had moved in, or if, maybe, one of the weatherman's servants would answer, Kate knocked on the tall, thick oak door.

"Coming. You're early." A muffled voice called. Then the door swung open, and S. J. Corbin's startled brown eyes stared at Kate.

twenty

Monday, July 17, 1950

EXTRA EDITION: JULIUS ROSENBERG ARRESTED.
The *Journal-American*'s headline almost leapt off the page.

Kate, who'd been following the spy case as religiously as she followed Cholly Knickerbocker's society gossip or Dorothy Kilgallen's *Voice of Broadway*, couldn't wait till she got home. She climbed onto a stool at Irv's counter, ordered a chocolate egg cream, and read every word of the story.

Not only was Mr. Rosenberg in a heap of trouble with the FBI, it looked like Mrs. Rosenberg, whose brother, David Greenglass, had named her husband as the man who'd recruited him to spy for the Soviet Union, might be arrested, too.

Even if Rosenbergs had been guilty—and, it sure read

like they were—what kind of man would betray his own family? A traitor trying to save his neck, she figured.

Kate had better get going; her mother wanted her to go through her old movie magazines and select only twenty to save. Mom had sounded serious, threatening that if Kate didn't do as requested, she'd throw them all out.

The clock behind the counter read two-thirty and Kate had to be at Sophie's at three-thirty. She ran the two blocks home.

"Katya," Mr. Provakov said, "please to try a piece of cake with your tea."

They'd reached the middle of *War and Peace*. Kate decided several chapters ago that the scenes set in Moscow, dealing with Natasha's romantic intrigue and social life, were far better than all those snowy battle scenes. Sophie had disagreed, saying the war reflected accurate Russian history and the romance was pure fiction. Kate preferred fiction; in fact, she'd also decided Margaret Mitchell's *Gone With the Wind*, her former favorite novel, had been heavily influenced by Tolstoy's *War and Peace*. The triangle of Nastasha, André, and Pierre, much like Scarlett, Rhett, and Ashley. And Napoleon's march much like Sherman's.

As her father poured the tea, Sophie said, "Maybe Mitchell did borrow some themes from Tolstoy."

Kate, sitting in an old, overstuffed, faded velvet chair under a Turkish carpet hanging on the wall, smiled, resisting the urge to say, I told you so. Instead, she reached for a slice of cake.

An afternoon tea break seemed as necessary to Mr. Provakov as it was to her mother and grandmother. Kate

liked that. One similarity in two very different house-
holds. No carpets hanging on her mother's walls.

For the most part, Kate and Sophie had explored and
enjoyed the differences. Irish soda bread and black bread
with lots of butter each had its own appeal. But some
foods were a problem. Borscht. The worst. Noodle pud-
ding. Ugh. Caviar. Double ugh.

Her mother was always after Kate to clean her plate,
unaware that she'd been putting peas in her pocket for
years, then flushing them down the toilet. She couldn't
chance that as a guest in the Provakov home, so she'd
been eating some mighty strange things. Sophie actually
loved beet soup. Kate's grandmother always said, "No ac-
counting for taste." Though Kate suspected that Etta had
been referring to people, not food.

Mr. Provakov stood. "Now is time for you young ladies
to get some fresh air. We exercise the brain; then we exercise the body. Walk up to the playground. Climb the monkey bars."

"Papa, they're for little children."

"Then jump rope. Please, you and Katya go now, yes. I
have work to do and I have a special dinner to prepare."

She loved being called, Katya. "My Kate." Mr.
Provakov had translated the term of endearment for her. It
made her feel like part of the family.

Kate had only met Sophie's mother, briefly, on two
Saturdays. Since Sophie's mother worked long hours as
a secretary, her father did the cooking, but he'd never
asked the girls to leave before. Were the Provakovs having company for dinner? If they were, Kate wished she'd
been invited.

As she reach for the doorknob, he spoke again. "Next
week, on Tuesday, is Sophie's thirteenth birthday. I'd like

to take you both to lunch at the Russian Tea Room. Katya, please ask your parents if you can be part of our celebration."

The Russian Tea Room. Holy smoke!

She'd read about its red velvet walls, its gilded sconces, and its Fifty-seventh Street location—"just a little to the left of Carnegie Hall"—in all the columns. No question, her mother would say yes. She'd die if her father said no.

Then she got to thinking about Marlene. They'd shared so many first adventures together, she felt funny that her former forever best friend wouldn't be part of this one. Sophie was great and she loved books and liked the movies, but she didn't giggle. Not ever. To tell the truth, she didn't laugh a lot. Kate's father had nicknamed her "Somber Sophie," saying she was a stodgy sixty-year-old masquerading in a twelve-year-old body. Kate had been most annoyed at him; she thanked God he never joked like that in front of Sophie. But there was something to be said for laughter. Kate really missed Marlene's giggle.

They walked up to the playground on Ninety-fifth Street. No one their age was hanging out there. No teenage boys playing basketball. Just little kids with their moms pushing their swings or waiting for them at the bottom of the slides. The sun felt warm, but a light breeze, hinting at rain, ruffled Kate's curls. She'd been so wrapped up in *War and Peace*, she'd lost track of where the boys were these days. Marlene would know.

"I have a dollar my grandmother gave me," Kate said. "Let's go to Irv's. We can each have an egg cream and I want to buy the latest *Modern Screen*."

"Okay," Sophie said, "Then I have to go home. My mother's bringing someone she works with home for dinner. He's been coming over a lot."

Just from the way Sophie spoke, Kate could tell dinner guests had been rare at the Provakov's.

Irv kidded Kate about two egg creams in one afternoon, and he didn't know about the tea and cake. Her mother would kill her if she didn't eat her dinner.

As they stepped out of the candy store, a real threat of rain was in the air. "I'll walk you home, Sophie. I don't dare bring another movie magazine into the house today."

"But it's almost six blocks out of your way. Just give me the magazine. I'll keep it until I see you again."

"No. I want to read about Liz Taylor and Nicky Hilton while we're walking."

Sophie shrugged.

Kate glanced up from the article as they turned right off Ninety-first Street and onto Thirty-fourth Avenue. "Just one more paragraph."

"We're here."

Kate, wondering if Liz and Nicky would be happy, handed Sophie the magazine. Out of the corner of her eye, she spotted Sophie's mother, dressed in a dark suit and a tall, gawky young man, at the entrance to Sophie's apartment house.

"Hello," Sophie called.

"Hi, Mrs. Provakov." Kate waved.

Sophie's mother looked startled; she turned away, fumbled with her key, yanked the heavy door open, motioning for the young man to precede her, then followed him into the lobby.

The rain came, pelting Kate's back.

No way had Sophie's mother not seen and heard them.

TWENTY·ONE

The Present

"You look like you just saw a ghost, S.J." Marlene sounded more amused than concerned. "We're the ones who should be startled. What are you doing here?"

"Waiting for a prospective buyer." Kate watched with fascination as S.J. took a deep breath and managed to regain her composure. "Are you ladies interested in upping his offer?"

"I thought Uncle Weatherwise sold his mansion before moving up to Ocean Vista." Kate forced a smile. "I assume you're acting as his Miami Realtor, too."

"Never assume anything, Kate. It makes an *ass* out of *u* and *me*."

"That joke's almost as old as we are, S.J." Marlene rolled her eyes. "As a cool South Beach player, you really ought to get some new material."

"You own the place, don't you?" Kate asked, once again certain the answer to her question would be yes. Had she turned into a mind reader?

"Why, yes, I do. " S.J. showed small, well-bonded teeth in a forced smile. "As I told you, Walt planned to move to the Southwest. With the way real estate's rocketing, when I heard he was selling all his Florida property, I put in an offer on the house on Tuesday, it was accepted by Walt's lawyer yesterday, and I have an eager buyer coming today." She sighed. "If it hadn't been for the hurricane, I probably would have turned it around already."

Strange. Kate had assumed—in an excellent example of why one should never assume anything—that Uncle Weatherwise had sold his South Beach mansion before moving to Palmetto Beach. And, according to Marlene, the condo board believed that, too. Of course, Bob, as finance chair and possibly Walt's business associate, might have known the truth.

"Dead sellers make good clients, right?" Marlene said. "No haggling."

S.J. blanched. "Weatherwise wasn't dead when I made the offer on this house."

"That's right," Marlene said, "but he was dead by the time his lawyer accepted it. And he was certainly dead, though that information hadn't gone public, when you made the offer on his Ocean Vista condo. Your real estate wheeling and dealing has left me a tad confused."

"Which one of you lovely ladies is Miss Corbin?" A voice behind Kate boomed.

"I'm S. J. Corbin," the Realtor smiled, pushing past Marlene and Kate, and extending her hand to a tall, middle-aged man in a white Stetson. "These ladies were just leaving."

"Well, good, cause I'm in a buying state of mind."

"The owner's not in his grave yet, and I hear the house is haunted," Marlene called over her shoulder as she walked toward the gate.

Kate laughed. "Okay, pull out your addresses. Let's start with Southern Trust and see what we can dig up on Bob Seeley."

Eager to get going, they decided not to eat in South Beach—and paid twenty-five bucks for valet parking without a voucher. It broke down to a dollar a minute.

The view from the causeway could convert even the most ardent Florida-phobe. The port of Miami's berths filled with beautiful cruise ships and ocean liners, Biscayne Bay's shores lined with gracious homes, the city skyline's tall buildings a gleaming tribute to the city's thriving commerce and industry, and the Atlantic Ocean, with white-capped waves and turquoise water as far as the eye could see.

Miami moved to a samba beat. The business district was crowded with cars, buses, cabs, and well-dressed pedestrians navigating the streets with style and purpose, both in short supply in Palmetto Beach.

The Southern Trust building stood taller than all the other downtown skyscrapers.

Kate entered its marble lobby, trying to project some style and compose herself. She'd better. On the way over the bridge, she and Marlene had concocted a script that required those attributes, plus a lot of lying.

A Playboy bunny posing as a receptionist sat at a desk that could have graced the Oval Office. "I'm sorry, Mr. Seeley retired three years ago. Moved north to the boonies."

"Yes, we know, but our friend, Walt Weatherwise, suggested we meet with the planner who's working with Mr. Seeley's former clients." Kate thought she'd delivered her line well.

The blonde mulled that over. "How about I get Mr. Moose. He took over most of Mr. Seeley's accounts."

Five minutes later, they were ushered into an office the size of small hotel's lobby. Mahogany desk and tables, Wedgwood lamps, dark oak floors, leather couches, and maroon velvet chairs. A veritable London men's club in the middle of Miami.

Mr. Moose, about thirty, slim, short, and perfectly turned out in Brooks Brothers, stood and greeted them with warmth. "I heard about Walt's death. My condolences on your friend's passing."

"Wonderful man." Marlene deadpanned. Kate had refused to utter that line.

"Do you ladies know Bob Seeley, too?"

"We hear he moved north to the boonies." Marlene improvised, not really lying. "We're Walt's neighbors here in South Beach. Er, we were, until his tragic passing." Now she was lying.

"Really?" The amazed look on the young man's face and the shock in his voice gratified Kate. If he bought into two old ladies living large in South Beach, they'd pull this charade off.

"I'm sorry, ladies, I didn't catch your names." Mr. Moose pulled out the two club chairs in front of his desk—as big as a New York studio—for them.

"I'm Barbara Stanwyck," Marlene said, "and this," she gestured to Kate, "is Marjorie Main."

Kate bit her lip. If Mr. Moose happened to be a fan of old movies, Marlene's ad lib would expose them. And leave it to her sister-in-law to grab star billing. She pictured the plain, erstwhile supporting actress, Marjorie Main—who'd played Ma Kettle back in the '50s—and wanted to wring Marlene's neck.

Moose remained clueless. "Please tell me how I can help you."

The delivery of the next line would be crucial. Kate took the lead. "We want to invest our money in the exact same portfolio Walt Weatherwise had. And, since you've taken over Bob Seeley's clients, we'd like you to be our financial planner."

Mr. Moose grinned. "Let's discuss that, ladies. For starters, I'm going to have Brittany serve you both a nice cup of tea while I pull up Walt's records."

While they sipped and smiled, an intense Mr. Moose reviewed Weatherwise's portfolio. After what felt like an eternity, he turned away from his computer, his expression blank.

Kate wished she could pop a Pepcid AC.

"I would recommend a much less aggressive approach than Mr. Seeley's for you ladies."

"Why?" Kate ventured, not knowing what else to say.

Moose frowned. "Well, without revealing either the amounts or the exact nature of the investments—and there hasn't been any trading over the last three years—I would advise you ladies to be more cautious, more diversified. Trading in options is risky business."

Perplexed, Kate said, "But Walt Weatherwise is a millionaire many times over, and we want to invest the same way he did."

"Ladies, please. When an investor agrees to take great risks, he can lose great amounts of money. Walt Weatherwise's portfolio didn't make a profit; in fact, it has sustained substantial losses."

So that was why Walt had been threatening Bob at the shelter. But Walt had millions; someone, maybe a previous financial planner, had made his money grow.

"Did Walt have another account here?" Marlene asked.

Mr. Moose shook his head. "Regrettably, no. Perhaps with another firm; however, I'm delighted that Walt sent you to us." He rubbed his palms together, and smiled. "Now, I'm going to custom-design the perfect portfolio for you lovely ladies."

Twenty·Two

"Options trading. I wonder what that is and if it can be manipulated?" Kate didn't hide her frustration or disappointment.

Marlene had parked the car in a nearby garage and, though dejected, they were both starving, and searched along the boulevard for a reasonable restaurant.

"How about this place?" Marlene pointed to a cute café, called Siesta.

Kate put on her glasses and read the menu posted next to the bright yellow door. "The price is right. Let's eat."

The Cuban-American waiter, better looking than any of the current crop of hot movie stars, served the "senoras" chicken with yellow rice and beans. Kate couldn't remember when she'd last enjoyed a meal as much as this one. And, having taken a prophylactic Pepcid AC, she could order the wonderful Cuban coffee and have the flan for dessert.

"You do have a financial planning expert in the family, you know; why don't you call her?" Marlene buttered her third piece of bread, not that Kate had eaten any less of the loaf.

"Funny how often you read my mind." Kate smiled. "I was just wondering if I should bother Jennifer at work."

Marlene handed Kate her cell phone.

Kate's firefighter son Kevin had married a Boston Brahmin. Jennifer Lowell. Blonde, beautiful, and brilliant. She'd just left Smith Barney to open her own investment firm on lower Park Avenue in New York City. Kate could live for a year on what Jennifer paid per month for her office space. She loved her daughter-in-law, who'd made her son happy and had given birth to Kate and Charlie's two wonderful granddaughters, Lauren, and Kate's namesake, Katharine. It was only that . . . well . . . Jennifer intimidated her . . . just a little.

"Press seven. That's Jennifer's new office number," Marlene said. "I'll order two coffees. Flan?"

Kate nodded, then followed Marlene's instructions.

The receptionist sounded like Grace Kelly in *High Society*. "Yes, Mrs. Kennedy, I'll tell Ms. Lowell you're calling." It bothered Kate—but just a little—that Jennifer didn't use her married name.

"Hi, Kate." Jennifer came across as warm, but busy. "How are you?"

"Fine. Look, I'm sorry to bother you at work, but I have a couple of quick financial questions, if you have the time."

"Sure. Shoot."

"If a broker or financial manager put most of a client's money into buying and selling options, but that client's portfolio now shows a loss, could there have been any way that the investor actually made a profit? Some way the broker might have manipulated the futures market or something?"

"A dishonest broker could," Jennifer said.

"How?" Kate's heart seemed to skip a beat. She should pass on the coffee, but she wouldn't.

"Let me make this as simple as possible. The broker could report selling an option low, when he'd actually sold high. Option profits can be enormous if the broker and the client are big enough gamblers. The trick would be to falsify the portfolio records to indicate a loss. The broker would have to be both clever and careful, cooking the books to avoid an auditor discovering the scheme."

How well do we really know our neighbors? Our friends? Our financial managers? Had fussy, refined Bob Seeley been a crook, who'd designed a complex stock fraud before he retired to Ocean Vista? "But where would the broker hide the money?"

Jennifer laughed. "Well, he could wire it to another account, say in a Swiss bank."

"How?"

"Oh, any number of ways. Use a fake name. Who knows, maybe the broker and the investor were partners in crime? Wouldn't be the first time."

Good God. Wouldn't this have been the exact information that Lucy Diamond had needed to indict Walt Weatherwise?

•   •   •

Ten minutes later, the matinee-idol waiter had served the coffee and dessert and Kate had caught Marlene up.

"So, you're saying Bob's smarter than Lucy? She'd have reviewed Weatherwise's portfolio with the best tax guys on the federal government's payroll, right?"

"What if she hadn't brought the Feds in? And, if she hadn't, why not? Because the auditors would have uncovered Bob's scam?" Kate sipped her coffee. "Could Lucy, despite all her histrionics to the contrary, have been protecting her former lover?"

"You said she'd been carrying a torch for Weatherwise. Maybe the flame hadn't gone out."

"Marlene, you're absolutely poetic." Kate smiled. "Now drink up; we need to get some background information on Lucy, and we have to decide where to start."

Marlene placed her empty demitasse cup on its saucer. "Ready to roll. The courthouse or the condo?"

"Well, we could probably walk to the courthouse, but how forthcoming are a bunch of federal prosecutors and their minions going to be? I vote for the condo. One of Lucy's former neighbors may be a chatterbox."

Kate signed the American Express receipt, leaving the hunk a 22 percent tip, and keeping the copy for her income tax deductions. Sure. She could list the lunch under amateur sleuth investigation expenses.

"But Lucy lived in Coral Gables. That's about fifteen minutes south of here. I thought we'd take I-95 home."

Kate had no intention of driving back to Palmetto Beach on the interstate with her sister-in-law at the wheel. "No, I like A1A a lot better. And what's another half-hour round-trip to Coral Gables in our unending quest for motive and murderer?"

Marlene laughed. "Now who's waxing poetic? Okay,

Kate, you win. We'll get the car out of the garage, drive down to the condo, and hope we get to interview a nosy neighbor."

On the way out of Siesta, Kate found herself sneaking one last look at the smiling waiter. She'd better behave or she might turn into Marlene.

twenty·three

Marlene was lying to the rent-a-cop stationed behind a window in the gatekeeper's booth.

Lucy's former residence had turned out to be in a condo community of bungalows, not unlike the old Hollywood bungalow colonies that Nathaniel West had immortalized. During the late thirties and early forties, many of the transplanted eastern writers, including F. Scott Fitzgerald and Dorothy Parker, who'd been brought to Los Angeles as script doctors, had lived in those small one-story houses with screened-in porches and casual charm.

"Sir, I assure you I have an appointment with a Realtor. The new owner in Lucy Diamond's former condo wants to sell." Marlene oozed charm.

"Mrs. Henratty? But she's gone up north for the summer."

A snowbird. They'd caught a break.

When the overweight, sixty-something guard could find no record of their names on his "to be admitted" list, Marlene blamed S. J. Corbin. "We're supposed to meet her here. I guess she's running late, but I'd really like to get in there and check out the grounds before she arrives." Marlene actually batted her eyelashes.

Marlene's boldfaced, if flawed, lies worked. Or maybe her flirting sealed the deal. The guard had heard of S. J. Corbin and, figuring there must have been a screwup in communication, raised the bar, and let them in. "Make a left off Rosebud Lane. It's the second bungalow on the right." Amazing. The poor guy was even giving them directions.

They drove through an enchanted garden-like setting. Bungalows, in Easter-egg colors, with kelly green lawns, circled an impressive white wooden clubhouse in much the same way that the Hollywood bungalows often had surrounded large, glamorous hotels. Off to the right, a golf course sloped down toward the Intercoastal.

"Enough of the sightseeing," Kate said. "The guard might wise up and come looking for us."

"Nah. I told you if we dressed to kill, we'd get away with murder." Marlene sounded annoyingly overconfident. "And we have so far, haven't we?"

"But . . ."

"Kate, in those pleated khakis and that white shirt, you look like Katharine Hepburn—well, when she was much older, of course."

What Marlene looked like defied description. An orange-red silk caftan over skintight purple silk tights. Maybe a tomato topping an eggplant, Kate decided, rather uncharitably. However, they were designer duds and, sometimes, that was all it took to crash South Florida society. Or a

SoBe mansion. Or Southern Trust's inner sanctum. Or a bungalow colony.

"Besides," Marlene said, giggling, "not to worry, I've besotted the guard."

Shades of Pete Blake. God, what had dredged up that memory? That name? Kate hadn't thought about Pete Blake in over fifty years. No, longer. Not since the summer of 1950. Sitting in the convertible, its top down and the warm afternoon sun on her face, she suddenly felt cold.

"What's the matter, Kate? You're shaking. Should I turn off the air-conditioning?"

"Yes, along with the engine. Park the car, Marlene. We have detective work to do."

Lucy's former cottage was painted the exact same shade of lilac as the flowers growing in its pristine, white-picket-fenced front yard. Upon closer inspection, Kate discovered the lilacs were plastic. What kind of a person would plant fake flowers? Obviously an owner who'd buy a bungalow in a condo community called End of the Rainbow.

"Yoo-hoo," a sweet voice called. "Are y'all looking for Cordelia Henratty?"

A pretty blonde, youngish woman, maybe in her late forties, dressed in a crisply pressed pale pink organdy blouse and matching pants, stood in the doorway of the pastel pink bungalow next door. At least she didn't have matching phony flowers in her garden. Those pink hibiscus were for real.

"We're looking for our old, dear friend, Lucy Diamond," Marlene said, sounding sweeter than the blonde neighbor. "Don't tell me she doesn't live here any longer."

"She sure doesn't."

"And we've driven all the way down from New York." Marlene segued from sweet to sad.

"Oh dear, Lucy moved out almost three years ago." If the woman wondered how they'd gotten past the guard, or why they would have driven all that distance without double-checking where their *old, dear friend* currently resided, she showed no curiosity. "Went up north to Palmetto Beach. I have her contact information in my address book. Why don't y'all come in for a glass of iced tea and I'll give it to you?"

Like stealing candy from a baby. Still, Kate felt no guilt and almost no shame as she followed the woman into the bungalow.

Lots of Laura Ashley fabric, needlepoint pillows, and oak shelves filled with dolls dressed in couture gowns. Mary Frances would love this living room. Kate rather liked it herself.

"I'm Daphne DuBois."

"I'm Stella and this is Blanche," Marlene said, pointing to Kate.

Kate cringed.

"Like the sisters in *A Streetcar Named Desire*? Don't tell me we share the same last name." Daphne, no dope, had gotten the bad joke.

"This is my friend, Marlene Friedman, who thinks she's funny. I'm Kate Kennedy." She said, blowing their cover, but not their cover story.

"Did you know Lucy well?" Marlene asked.

Kate, not trusting Marlene to act as inquisitor, jumped in. "We've been worried about Lucy. Last we heard, she'd been dating a man who broke her heart." Just enough truth to make them seem credible, Kate hoped.

"Oh, you mean Walt, the weatherman. A dirty hound dog. But he didn't break Lucy's heart."

"He didn't?" Kate didn't have to feign surprise.

"She hated Walt; she only flirted to try and get the goods on him. She wanted him behind bars. Or worse. Y'all have to understand Lucy was obsessed, and her thirst for revenge seemed to go way back, though she never explained why. Or discussed what he'd done. How many times she'd say, over a scotch, 'I'd sleep with the devil himself, if it would help me send him to hell.'"

twenty·four

"And everywhere that Nicky went, the snoops were sure to go."

Kate and Marlene, full of iced tea and food for thought, had expressed gratitude to their hostess, closed the bungalow's rose-colored front door, and were squinting in the bright sunshine.

Nick Carbone, yet again catching them playing detective, sounded fed up and furious. And unnecessarily snide, Kate thought, though she couldn't come up with a response.

Marlene mumbled, "Sorry," clearly not apologizing for snooping, but regretting she hadn't gotten away with it.

"I've been one step behind since your visit to Weatherwise's place in SoBe. You two old broads really snowed young Mr. Moose. He had no idea you'd graduated summa cum laude from Miss Marple's campus in St. Whatever-the-hell-village she lived in. I'd have made it here before you, but I miscalculated your game plan and stopped by the courthouse first."

"Bet we learned more by coming straight here. Always go with neighbors before coworkers," Marlene said, in a smart-aleck tone that used to drive Charlie crazy.

Kate wanted to kick her, but couldn't with Carbone watching their every move.

"Listen, Marlene," Nick said, "you're about one word away from being arrested for impeding a police investigation." His face flushed scarlet and a vein bulged at his temple.

"We're on our way home." Kate grabbed Marlene's arm. She considered adding "We were only trying to help," but since he appeared ready to burst a blood vessel, she figured they should just get out of his sight. As quickly as possible.

The detective strode past them and knocked on Daphne's door. Feeling guilty and, yes, sorry, Kate wondered if he'd ask the right questions.

"Are you mad at me?" Marlene asked.

They'd compromised and were driving home on Federal Highway. Not a smart decision. The traffic, with almost as many trucks as I-95, had come to a complete halt.

In the hot afternoon sun, they had the convertible's top up and the air on full blast.

"Must be an accident ahead," Kate said, ignoring Marlene's question. She did feel angry. Marlene always chose the damnedest times to assert herself, with no regard for the consequences. "Maybe we should get off and take the beach road."

"I'll try to get in the right lane as soon as the traffic starts moving, and we'll head east." Marlene managed to sound both conciliatory and impatient. "Are you annoyed because I aggravated Nick Carbone?"

Marlene wasn't going to drop it. "Well, yes, weren't we in enough trouble without you raising his blood pressure?"

"Don't worry, Kate. He still likes you. You could be dating him if . . ."

"If what?" The words spilled out before she could edit them. Leave it to Marlene to twist things around. And why had Kate just given her diversion credence?

"If you'd just get over Charlie and open yourself up to new experiences."

"You don't just get over forty-six years, Marlene. It's not like the flu." Kate's voice broke. She bit her lip, wishing she were anywhere except trapped in traffic with her sister-in-law.

"Okay, you're right. I was out of line. I'll call Carbone and apologize . . . for real." She reached over and patted Kate's knee. "And I'm sorry if I upset you. You know I only want you to be happy."

As she'd done for decades, Kate decided to move on. Sometimes she wondered if there would ever be a time when she couldn't forgive Marlene. What would happen? How would Marlene handle it? How would Kate?

For now, Kate nodded.

And Marlene, as she'd done for decades, changed the subject. "So was Lucy Diamond a woman spurned or a woman obsessed? Either way the result would have been the same. She wanted Weatherwise in jail, right?"

"The result might have been the same, but not the motivation. Why would Lucy tell me that sad story of unrequited love? Why wouldn't she have told me that she'd duped Walt and only flirted to set him up? Why stage a performance to convince me otherwise?"

"Strange." Marlene veered into the right lane.

"Maybe not. If Lucy's motive for seducing then turning on Weatherwise had preceded his financial shenanigans in Miami, perhaps Lucy had reason to hide that motive."

"Or maybe Daphne had been misinformed—or, for some reason, misinformed us—about Lucy and Walt's relationship."

Kate shook her head. "I don't think so. I had a feeling that Lucy was acting in my apartment last night. That she acts a lot."

At the next light, Marlene made a right and headed east toward the beach. "She's an attorney. They're all actors."

"Well, Bob Seeley deserves an Academy Award. He never let on he'd known Weatherwise before he moved to Ocean Vista, never mind that his bad advice had cost the weatherman millions of dollars."

"Or not," Marlene said. "More likely those two old crooks made millions, then stashed the dough in an off-shore account, even if Lucy couldn't prove it."

"That's the real mystery," Kate said. "Why couldn't she prove it?"

The opening bars of *As Time Goes By* filled the convertible. Kate grabbed her bag and scrambled to find her cell phone. "Hi, this is Kate Kennedy."

"Kate, it's Mary Frances."

Kate whispered to Marlene, "Mary Frances."

"I'm wondering where you are right now."

"Marlene and I are driving up A1A, heading home from Miami." Kate peered out the window. The sea had turned navy blue and the waves looked rough. "We're about fifteen minutes south of Hollywood Beach."

"Good. Thank God," Mary Frances sighed. "Do you think you could pick me up at the airport? You're only about thirty minutes away. I can wait."

"What? You mean Fort Lauderdale Airport? You're home?"

"She's here?" Marlene asked.

Kate waved a hand to silence her.

"Yes, I called Joe Sajak, but he's up in Palm Beach." Mary Frances sounded sad, on the verge of tears. "Could you please come get me? Northwest Airlines terminal. Please."

"We're on our way, "Kate said.

Marlene groaned.

"Oh," Mary Frances said, "do you have the radio on?"

Puzzled, Kate said, "No. Why?"

"Turn it on. They predicting another hurricane. And saying it could be as bad as Andrew."

Twenty·Five

Monday, July 24, 1950

It was inevitable—Kate's new favorite word—that she'd run into Marlene. Jackson Heights might be part of New York City, but it was a neighborhood, their neighborhood. Of course, Marlene lived right next door, but Kate just *knew* they'd be destined to meet in the lobby of one of the town's five movie theaters. It turned out to be their least favorite, the Polk.

On Monday nights, the Polk Theater gave away free dishes. One per customer. Maggie never missed, often dragging Kate and Etta along, so they could bring home three cereal bowls. Kate figured if they all attended B movies every Monday night for the next twenty years, her mother might end up with service for twelve. Maggie, however, took a more optimistic point of view. "Just one more cup and two more saucers and I can serve four people tea."

"Oh, Mom, do I really have to go?" Kate knew her protest wouldn't deter Maggie from her mission. Her mother had fallen in love with those god-awful, ugly, olive-green dishes. And her grandmother had begged off, citing one of her bilious attacks, a vague stomach complaint that Kate had long suspected occurred on cue when Etta didn't want to do something.

"Yes. Bread-and-butter plates, tonight." Her mother shook, then folded the tablecloth. "Go brush your teeth and change your blouse. We're leaving in ten minutes."

"What's wrong with my blouse?" Kate loved her ruffled, peasant blouse. She always loosened the drawstring at the neckline and dropped the sleeves off her shoulders as soon as she left the house.

"It's too bare. The movie is air-conditioned, Kate. A shirtwaist would be better."

Kate suspected the air-conditioning had little to do with why her mother had dictated what her daughter should wear. Living with Maggie Norton was like living under Stalin.

Ladies from Corona, in cotton, flower-patterned housedresses, cluttered the small lobby. The Polk, on Thirty-seventh Avenue and Ninety-fourth Street, was only a short walk from Junction Boulevard, the dividing line between Jackson Heights and Corona.

Kate stared at the bow in the back of one woman's apron-like dress. And her mother had been worried about Kate's peasant blouse.

"Give me a break, Mom. That lady over there with the tight perm looks like a field of lilies on parade."

"Lower your voice, Katharine. It's rude to comment on what other people wear."

"Never stopped you, Mom."

"Enough." Her mother sounded annoyed, but her blue eyes were smiling. "Do you want a box of nonpareils?"

A peace offering. Kate loved the little chocolate drops, topped with white sprinkles.

"Sure. Thanks."

Standing in front of the narrow counter at the refreshment stand, Kate ordered, then felt a poke in the middle of her spine. "It's good to see your favorite candy hasn't changed." Marlene's laughter filled the small lobby.

She spun around, smiling, saying, "Hi, Marlene," her voice tinny.

"I'm here as a stand-in for my mother. She and my dad are sitting with the dead. Well, with my aunt, who's alive; it's my uncle who's dead. I'm excused tonight to get Mom a bread-and-butter plate."

"I'm sorry for your loss, Marlene," Maggie said. "Your father's sister's husband, right? I heard he'd been ill. Please give your parents my condolences."

Kate could almost hear the click in her mother's brain, as she made a mental note to buy a sympathy card. Emily Post was Maggie Norton's favorite columnist. Mom often started sentences, "According to Emily Post," and finished them with, "and that certainly applies to you, Kate."

"My mother thought you could walk me home, Mrs. Norton," Marlene said, almost hesitantly.

"Of course, Marlene," Maggie said, "and you'll sit with us, too. Now how about a Milky Way? That's your favorite, isn't it?"

Midway through the coming attractions, Marlene had Kate laughing. They whispered during the Three Stooges short, since neither the girls nor Maggie could stand the slapstick routines. By the time they reached the lobby, dissecting *Destination Moon*, the better of the two B pictures, they'd decided to fly to the moon when they grew up, figuring space travel would be as accessible as the IRT.

They stepped out of air-conditioning and into humidity. Kate could feel her hair turn to frizz. With her mother in the middle, they walked three abreast on the avenue.

Marlene, who'd grown quiet, mumbled, "I'm sorry, Kate. I acted like a real jerk with Pete Blake, who turned out to be a skunk."

How about that? An apology. Out of the blue. Or maybe not. The pleased smile lighting up her mother's face made Kate wonder if the entire evening had been a set up.

"How about an ice cream soda at Wolke's, kind of a nightcap?" Maggie asked.

Any other time Kate would have jumped at the invitation, but she wanted to get home and wash her hair. Her curls were out of control. She had a luncheon engagement with Mr. Provakov and Sophie at the Russian Tea Room tomorrow. How Cholly Knickerbocker was that? Their estimated time of departure from Queens was 11:30 A.M. Kate wanted her mother to set those stubborn curls in bobby pins; then she'd keep the pins in overnight, and wake up with waves. Still, if she didn't go for a soda, Marlene would think she hadn't accepted her apology.

"Great," Kate said, thinking she'd have to get up at the crack of dawn to wash and dry her hair.

Marlene seemed so pleased to be going to the ice

cream parlor that Kate decided the inconvenience *might* be worth it. But if her hair looked fuzzy tomorrow, she *might* change her mind.

Wolke's was located next to Brady's, an Irish bar and grill on Ninetieth Street, steps away from the entrance to the subway on Roosevelt Avenue. Weary office workers could come down the staircase, make a right, and pop into Brady's for a cocktail or a beer before heading home. The Norton family often ate dinner there on Friday nights. Delicious filet of sole, French fries, and cole slaw.

As Kate followed her mother and Marlene into the ice cream parlor, she noticed a man and a woman leaving the bar. She stopped short. The woman was Sophie's mother. The tall, younger man was the same guy who'd been with Mrs. Provakov last week at her apartment house door when she'd ignored Sophie and Kate.

Good God! Could Mrs. Provakov be like Lana Turner in *The Postman Always Rings Twice*? Or Barbara Stanwyck in *Double Indemnity*? Could Sophie's mother be having an affair?

TWenTY·six

Tuesday, July 25, 1950

"Get your head out of the oven," her mother screamed.

Kate, drying her hair on low heat, was kneeling, her face resting on arms spread across the open oven door. She scrambled backward to get up.

"Have you gone crazy, Kate?" Maggie sounded like that might be a real possibility.

"My hair's still wet, Mom. If it doesn't dry before I leave, I'll be the only fuzz-head in the Russian Tea Room."

"We have almost two hours. Come on, we'll towel-dry it and I'll set it in bobby pins, then we'll have a nice cup of tea." Her mother rubbed Kate's arm. "You'll have soft curls, honey, I promise."

"I want waves." Kate whined. Tired. Cranky. Anxious. She was behaving like a spoiled six-year-old. "Sorry, Mom. Thanks. Let's get started."

Maggie Norton worked magic. No waves, but Kate's chestnut curls appeared glossy and smooth, not frizzy or dry. She liked the way they framed her face. And her mother said lots of young women would kill for those curls, for that thick hair.

Over tea, her mother had drilled Kate on table manners, focusing this morning on place settings. "Start with the fork farthest away from the plate." She just nodded, though she could recite her mother's Emily Post routine, chapter and verse.

Kate left the house feeling pretty good about herself. She wore a favorite sundress, dark green with a full skirt, and a white-trimmed bolero jacket, white, open-toe wedgies, and carried a matching bag. Best of all, Mom had made her up. A smudge of eye shadow made her green eyes bigger and brighter. A swipe of color on her cheeks, a light coating of coral lipstick, and her nails matched her lips. She'd bet she could pass for sixteen. Well, maybe, fifteen.

Sophie and her father were waiting for her at the bus stop on Ninetieth Street and Thirty-fourth Avenue. They'd ride to the Seventy-fourth Street terminal, then take the F train to the city.

Mr. Provakov appeared much more foreign in his well-worn tweed jacket, way too warm and out of season for the summer day. And the man had on Hush Puppies; his feet must be sweating. Could that be why his wife was seeing another man? Kate banished that idea. After all, Mrs. Provakov could have stayed late at the office, then stopped for a drink or a snack with her coworker.

She turned her attention to Sophie, who looked like the cover of *Seventeen*, in a fitted, chocolate brown linen dress and matching patent leather sandals, her dark hair pulled into a loose twist at the nape of her neck.

Kate suddenly felt as out of style as Sophie's father.

In the silence that had prevailed through most of the trip, they walked down the south side of Fifty-seventh Street. A canopy with big, bold, block letters signaled their arrival at the Russian Tea Room, slightly to the left of Carnegie Hall. Only the Rembrandt Building, that housed the Casino Russe, a Russian nightclub, stood between the restaurant and the concert hall. Kate once had seen a photograph of Yul Brynner sitting cross-legged at his sister's feet, playing the balalaika in the casino.

Above a patch of black-and-white-checkered sidewalk, brass panels bracketed the restaurant's revolving glass door. A menu in the window, displayed like a piece of precious Russian art, offered exotic fare, like zakuska, pojarsky cotelettes, and luli kebab.

Kate could hear her heart pounding and feel her palms go clammy. She was about to enter a world she'd only read about, a world she yearned to see, touch, savor, and remember. She promised herself to order a dish she'd never tried, then giggled. That should pose no problem here.

"Something is amusing, Katya?" Mr. Provakov sounded gentle. Concerned.

"No, nothing. I'm just happy to be here." Thrilled, actually. Kate sensed that Sophie and her father didn't share her enthusiasm. Why? Here they were in the middle of Manhattan, about to celebrate Sophie's thirteenth birthday in one of the city's most famous restaurants. Why wouldn't they be happy?

Mr. Provakov pushed the revolving door, followed by Sophie and Kate. They entered a red-and-gold room, unlike any Kate had ever seen, filled with huge urns holding spectacular flower arrangements, crystal decanters, and beautiful oil paintings. The long bar on the right had four red leather stools, matching the cushioned booths on the left.

Kate smiled. What a neat place. "Wow!"

Sophie nodded. "Even more than I expected."

Behind a partition at the end of the bar, Kate could see the dining room. Red walls. Brass-trimmed, enormous, low-hanging chandeliers sparkled like jewels. Shelves held silver samovars. Tables, with their pretty pink cloths and napkins, were surrounded by more beautiful paintings.

A mustached waiter in a Russian tunic seated them. Kate felt overwhelmed, as if she'd entered a fairyland filed with grown-ups in business suits. "The young ladies, please to sit here." The waiter pulled out two chairs at a table near the center of the dining room. "You can see my favorite mural while you eat." The mural of two ballet dancers, the man lifting the woman into the air, delighted Kate.

Though nervous, she took Mr. Provakov's suggestion and ordered the bilini with sour cream and caviar. The latter was so salty she wanted to spit it out. Maybe just having learned that caviar was made from fish eggs had colored her taste buds.

In such a festive setting and with such attentive service, Kate again puzzled over the lack of laughter or even good conversation. Both Mr. Provakov and Sophie seemed preoccupied.

Over a delicious Charlotte Russe and dark, thick, hot tea, served in a tall crystal glass with a sterling silver holder, she gave Sophie her birthday present.

Kate and her mother had shopped in New York City for two full afternoons, finally agreeing they'd found the perfect gift: a hammered silver Russian-style cross on a sterling silver chain. They bought it in a jewelry store near the Park Sheraton Hotel and her fathers office, and not far from the Russian Tea Room. Her mother had wrapped the box in silver paper and tied it with a baby blue satin ribbon. And Kate had searched for, and bought, what she considered a perfect, not corny, birthday card.

But now, as she fumbled in her bag, then handed Sophie the card and the present, Kate was no longer sure they were perfect.

"This is very kind of you, Kate." Sophie said with no conviction, barely glancing at the card. "I'll put it on right now."

The waiter brought Mr. Provakov another vodka, and more tea and dessert for all of them.

"Will you please help me with the clasp, Kate?" Sophie asked, struggling with the two ends of the chain.

Kate stood behind Sophie's chair, closed the clasp, then sat, and dug into her second Charlotte Russe. The ballet dancers seemed to be looking down at her and laughing.

A dark-haired middle-aged woman, dressed in a navy blue suit, averted her eyes as she passed by their table.

"Katya," Mr. Provakov said, "will you do me a great favor?" He reached into his baggy jacket's inside pocket and pulled out a white, sealed envelope. "Would you please deliver this note to the dark-haired lady who just went to the ladies room?"

Kate froze, a forkful of Charlotte Russe halfway to her mouth, and stared at him. "Now?"

"Yes. Our little secret, Katya. The lady is a cousin of

my wife's. They have had a falling out. In the note, my wife apologizes."

As he handed her the envelope, Kate wondered how Mr. Provakov had known his wife's cousin would be at the restaurant. And why Sophie couldn't have delivered it.

In the gilt-and-gold ladies room, the woman smiled warmly when Kate offered her the envelope, then took it without a word, and turned away. Kate met her eyes, reflected in a mirror. In those dark eyes, Kate saw fear and sorrow. And she looked so familiar.

Kate started, trying to swallow a scream. She'd seen that face in the newspapers.

The woman bolted into a stall.

Oh, my God! She was in the bathroom with Ethel Rosenberg.

twenty·seven

The Present

Mary Frances seemed determined to cry all the way to Ocean Vista. And on the radio, the broadcasters all cried hurricane.

Kate didn't scoff; the weather service might have been off by miles with Harriet, but most of the time they got it right. Igor wasn't due to land for several days, but he was picking up speed and, right now, they were predicting the greater Fort Lauderdale area would be ground zero. If Igor stayed on course, they'd be evacuating A1A from Miami to Palm Beach.

"Enough, already. This time *I'm* going down with condo," Marlene said, then turned to Kate. "Hand the weeper a tissue, will you?"

Kate reached into her bag and did as instructed.

Marlene beeped at the driver in front of her as the

Neptune Boulevard Bridge came down and locked into place. "Move it, buddy!"

The driver gave her the finger.

Marlene retaliated, then whirled around to face the backseat. "And, for God's sake, Mary Frances, stop that sniveling. Joe Sajak isn't worth your tears, never mind your virginity."

Kate had to laugh.

"What's so funny, Kate?" Mary Frances asked, then blew her nose for what seemed to be the hundredth time. "I need more tissues."

"Okay, but this is the last of my Kleenex." Kate parted with the packet reluctantly. She felt insecure without her supply of tissues and Pepcid AC. But she was worried. Mary Frances, always so perfectly turned out, looked like hell: her Maureen O'Hara red hair disheveled, her khaki pantsuit wrinkled, and her beautiful face, minus makeup, revealing sags and wrinkles that Kate had never noticed before.

"Marlene, are you sure Joe has been seeing another woman?" Mary Frances gulped.

"Make that plural, sweetie," Marlene said. "The man fancies himself a lady-killer. If you don't believe me, just ask Rosie O'Grady. She's seen Sajak in action at Ireland's Inn, too."

"Is Lucy one of his paramours?" The former nun came across like the schoolteacher she'd once been.

"Paramours?" Marlene roared. "You make Sajak sound like Louis the Fourteenth."

Good God. Could Joe be having an affair with Lucy? "Why do you ask that, Mary Frances?" Kate poked Marlene, hoping she'd get the message and keep quiet.

"Because, Joe serves on Lucy's bylaws committee."

Mary Frances sobbed. "The two of them are rewriting an entire section, about not letting kids under three in the pool. The diaper issue. A real hot button. He's been *working* at her place till all hours of the morning."

Marlene kept her eyes on the bridge and her mouth shut. Kate, figuring that wouldn't last long, changed the subject. "How about when we get home we change our clothes and take Ballou for a nice long walk on the beach?" Kate had been worrying about the Westie, home alone all day. And if Mary Frances tagged along on his outing, Kate could pump her. The former nun might know much more than she realized about Lucy Diamond, unlikely temptress and proven liar. "Maybe we can go to the pier and have the shrimp dinner at the Neptune Inn."

"There's a hurricane coming, Kate," Mary Frances said.

"Oh, not for days. We have lots of time to get ready." Why was she so driven to solve these murders? The need felt personal, physical, like an unquenchable thirst. But why? She hardly knew the victims. And what little she'd known about them she hadn't liked.

Marlene pulled into Ocean Vista's parking lot. Cops filled every corner. A tow truck, attached to Rosie O'Grady's Lincoln, was headed toward the exit. Rosie protested loud enough to be heard in Cleveland. No one responded. A young policeman waved Marlene to the far end of the lot, next to the fence on the beach side. They lucked out—a snow bird's spot was empty; otherwise they'd have been driving up and down Palmetto Beach's side streets for hours, trying to find a place to park.

Rosie ran after the truck, yelling, "Stop, thief."

If Rosie weren't so frantic and appearing so vulnerable in a faded blue robe, it might have been a funny scene. Instead, Kate felt outraged. Where was Carbone? Why hadn't he been here to oversee this mess?

"Can they seize her car like that? Isn't she protected under the Bill of Rights?" Mary Frances demanded, as they hurried toward Rosie, who was hurling expletives at the tow truck driver.

"It's a crime scene," Kate said. "They need to process the evidence."

Marlene reached Rosie first, putting an arm around her.

"I'm marooned here without my car, Marlene. They've stolen my independence and they won't even tell me when I'll get it back." Rosie sobbed. "And God knows my Lincoln will never be the same after them bums get finished ripping out its guts."

"You'll come with us to dinner at Herb's tonight," Kate said. "And I'm going to call Nick Carbone and tell him that you need your car returned as soon as possible."

"Fat lot of good that'll do," Rosie said. "When are we eating?"

One of Palmetto Beach's finest winked at Kate.

Marlene and a bit more mellow Rosie led the way into the lobby with Mary Frances, who'd stopped crying, and Kate trailing behind.

"Good afternoon, ladies." Miss Miford checked her watch. "Welcome home, Miss Costello. " Mitford moved on. "Ms. Friedman, the other board members have been trying to contact you to discuss hurricane emergency preparations. Both Mr. Seeley and Ms. Diamond asked me to call them the minute you showed up."

"Oh, hell," Marlene said. "I'll be tied up for a while. I'll catch up with you later at Herb's."

"As vice president, shouldn't I be included in the discussions?" Mary Frances asked.

"Yeah, yeah, I guess so," Marlene said, checking her watch. "It's five-thirty now. First, I'm going to shower and change. Then I'll call a quick meeting. Mary Frances and I will try to be at the Neptune Inn by seven. Get a table with an ocean view and order me a double martini."

Kate sighed. Damn, after all her great plans to question Mary Frances, she'd be stuck with Rosie.

A very excited Westie jumped up, almost making Kate lose her balance, then jumped again, licking her hand. "I love you, too, Ballou. Now, if you behave and be patient a little longer, you're going out to dinner with me and Rosie O'Grady." Kate didn't dare say *walk* or she'd never get into the shower.

Throughout her toilette, a matinee-idol, thirty-something weatherman—Weatherwise's replacement?—kept updating dire predictions of a Category Three Igor, turning into a Category Four, then heading in a direct path toward Fort Lauderdale. The young man's words chilled, yet annoyed, her.

By six-fifteen, Kate, Rosie, and Ballou were on the beach, walking north toward the Neptune Boulevard Pier. White-capped navy blue waves rolled ashore a few feet away. The sky, as muted as an impressionist painting, brushed against the horizon.

The happy Westie led the way, pulling Kate along. Ballou's happiness proved to be contagious. Kate's mood improved. She couldn't question Mary Frances about Lucy Diamond, but she could get some answers from Rosie. Make a few waves of her own.

And she wouldn't pussyfoot around. "Rosie, someone told me you had a weather vane in your tote bag on the night Weatherwise was murdered. Is that true?"

"Son of a gun. Old big-mouth pansy Bob, told you that, didn't he?"

"Yes." In for a dime, in for a dollar. "Is it true?" Kate tried to rein in Ballou, who'd picked up his pace.

"Yes, damn it, it's true. I saw Bob poking around my stuff. Do you suppose he told the police, too?"

Well, if Bob had told Lee Parker, Rosie would have had good reason to want the detective dead. Wait . . . she'd have needed Bob dead, too. "I don't know, but somehow, I don't think so."

"Damn. And double damn." Rosie kicked a pile of sand, sending it flying.

Ballou yelped with indignation.

"Why did you have the murder weapon in your tote bag?"

"See," Rosie spoke through her teeth, "that's why I didn't tell nobody. You right away jumped to the conclusion that, because I had a weather vane in my bag, I musta killed Weatherwise. I didn't know it was a weapon, did I?"

Kate waited.

"Walt asked me to hold it for him. When we was on the bridge, crossing to the mainland. He couldn't hold the weather vane and hang on to the rope. I put it in my tote bag." Rosie shook her head. "Someone must have spotted it at the shelter later and decided it would make the perfect murder weapon."

So maybe, if Rosie spoke the truth, Weatherwise's murder hadn't been premeditated. "Any idea who that someone might be?"

"Well, duh, his cheating business partner, Bob Seeley."

twenty·eight

"A double scotch old-fashioned, no sugar, light on the bitters, a dash of club soda, muddle well, especially the orange, and no cherry."

"You should carry a card with those instructions, Rosie." Herb said, laughing. "Good thing I'm tending bar tonight. You'd drive a lesser man to drink."

"I've driven many men to worse things than drink," Rosie said.

Kate had no doubt.

The Neptune Inn had been her favorite restaurant since before Charlie died. When they'd visited Marlene, Kate and Charlie had always eaten at Herb's. The six-six, three-hundred-pound owner's big heart and warm, welcoming personality had made the Neptune Inn a standout in a beach town filled with good restaurants. Its location on the pier with a great view of the Atlantic didn't hurt business either. And Kate believed Herb served the best fried shrimp platter in South Florida.

They were sitting on backless stools that would have damaged an agile teenager's spine. What had Herb done with the old leather stools that were more like director chairs?

Kate had hoped to entice Rosie to a table where she could question her in privacy, but the former Rockette insisted on having a "cocktail or two" at the bar. Should she start now? Rosie didn't appear to be having trouble with the uncomfortable seats. And, except for a few surfers, they wasn't anyone else at the bar.

"Igor could be our Katrina." The young weatherman, on the oversized television screen positioned above the bar, smiled as he predicted disaster. "Enormous waves, followed by flooding in the coastal communities." One of the surfers applauded the possibility.

Kate, repelled by both the weatherman and the bleached-blond beach boy chugging a Long Island ice tea, turned her attention to Rosie and what she might know about Bob Seeley's past. "Rosie, I suspect Bob might have been hiding Weatherwise's money in an overseas bank account. If you have any knowledge—or proof—of that, you really should tell Nick Carbone."

"Me? Talk to the cops? Whadda ya crazy?"

"You wouldn't want Bob to get away with murder, would you?"

"Jeez, no." Rosie drained her old-fashioned. "But I can't go the cops. I can't reveal my source."

How Woodward and Bernstein. "Your source?" What information did Rosie have? And, more intriguingly, how had she gotten it?

"Herb, hit me again. You want another white wine, Kate? This round's on me."

Kate didn't want any more wine, as she was so tired she might fall off the bar stool, but she said, "Thanks."

Ballou had his head on her left foot. Kate, seated under an air-conditioning vent, appreciated his furry warmth.

Rosie said nothing until her cocktail arrived, then she took a long sip and faced Kate. "Okay, I'm gonna trust you. Here's why I can't talk. A wiseguy I used to date in New York—high up in the mob, a capo—now lives in Boca. Quite the gentleman, has a big, fancy house on a golf course. I still see him once in a while. You know, a little roll in the hay for old time's sake. Anyway, Bob was my friend's financial planner. Seeley made some smart investments, adjusted a few statements, and, guess what? The wiseguys profits are an offshore account. Way off shore. Like Switzerland."

"Bob Seeley has mob connections?"

"Are ya deaf or just dumb?" Rosie shook her head.

Kate almost lost her balance, knocking Ballou off her foot. The Westie yelped with indignation. "He seems so meek. Such a mild manner."

"Mild manner, my foot. He may look like a scrawny, old guy, but Bob Seeley was a U.S. Army Ranger, trained in the martial arts. He's still pretty strong. I saw him at Gold's Gym. Works out there three times a week. I sure as hell didn't give Parker a karate chop, but Bob could have."

Kate remembered the pressed pajamas. Bob hadn't been sleeping as he'd claimed, but he hadn't been covered in blood either. Of course, he could have changed. Or, maybe the killer had worn a plastic cape—or some sort of cover-up—and took it with him or her.

"Where's my double martini?" Marlene asked, startling

Kate. "Herb, my friends have forgotten to order me a drink, and I really need one."

"One double martini coming up," Herb said, smiling at Mary Frances. "Nice to see you back home."

Mary Frances looked as harried as Marlene sounded.

"We're holding an emergency board meeting at ten o'clock tomorrow morning to plan Ocean Vista's evacuation. Bob and Lucy are putting notices under everyone's doors as we speak. I told them Mary Frances and I had an important engagement, so we couldn't help." Marlene sighed. "Damn, I wish I hadn't given up smoking."

"Since when?" Kate asked, remembering Marlene had smoked at lunch and after they'd met Mr. Moose and again after visiting Daphne Dubois.

"Since I ran out of cigarettes before the meeting." Marlene shrugged. "I figured if I could sit through that without going crazy, I don't need tobacco anymore. Of course, I may go back."

Rosie pulled out a package of Virginia Slims and lit up. Should be a fun dinner.

"Kate, did you and Rosie see Joe Sajak around?" Mary Frances asked. "On the beach or the pier?"

"I thought you went back into the convent, Mary Frances," Rosie said. "Why are so interested in Joe's whereabouts? In fact, if you're a nun again, whadda ya doing here? Did ya come for your dolls?"

A really fun dinner. "Shall we go to our table?" Kate asked with as much enthusiasm as she could muster.

"For your information, Rosie, I have not reentered the convent, I've been on retreat. Reflection, prayer, and mediation," Mary Frances said. "Good for your soul."

Rosie winked. "But not for your body."

The television weatherman screeched, "Igor has picked up more wind. This hurricane could be our biggest ever."

Rosie pointed her cigarette at Mary Frances. "Jest so ya know, sister, Joe's going dancing with me tonight at Ireland's Inn."

"I thought Joe was interested in Lucy." Mary Frances's voice shook. She flushed the feverishly bright pink that only redheads can, from the nape of her neck to her hairline.

"Nah," Rosie said, "I'd have heard if he was seeing Lucy. He ain't interested in me, either. " Rosie seemed rueful, but kinder, willing to swap girl talk. Eighty-four-year-old girl talk. "Sajak plays the field. Fancies himself quite the catch. If you're out of the convent and on the make, you could do a lot better than him, Mary Frances."

To Kate's surprise, Mary Frances nodded, seeming to consider Rosie's advice.

When they finally ordered, Rosie, finishing her third old-fashioned, reminisced about her Radio City dancing days. "Cocktails at Twenty One. Dinner at Tavern on the Green. Supper at the Copa. Those were the days, my friends. I loved the Mermaid Lounge at the Park Sheraton. Any of you gals been there? Well, you New York gals, not Miss Minnesota, here." Rosie gestured at Mary Frances.

"Wisconsin," Mary Frances said.

"It's all the same." Rosie waved Herb over. "Another round, please."

"Not for me, thanks, Herb," Kate said. "You know, I do remember the Mermaid Lounge. My father took me there to hear Cy Coleman. The summer I turned thirteen." The sudden flashback jarred her. She'd forgotten her visit to the Park Sheraton, having tucked it away in a seldom-visited, never-examined corner of her mind, along with other, more disturbing memories from that long ago summer.

"Hello, Kate," a cheerful voice said. Dazed, she looked up into the smiling face of S. J. Corbin. "How are all you ladies doing?"

"Why don't ya join us for a drink, S.J.?" Rosie asked.

"I'm sorry, I'm meeting Joe Sajak for dinner, but I'll take a rain check." The Realtor extended her hand to Mary Frances. "I don't believe we've met. I'm S. J. Corbin."

Mary Frances stared at S.J., saying nothing, looking like a startled doe.

Kate shook off her past, and turned toward S.J., smartly dressed in a black linen jumpsuit. "Another time, then."

"I'll count on that, Kate." She fingered a chain around her neck, adjusting the hammered silver Russian cross hanging from it.

twenty·nine

Friday, July 28, 1950

What was in the envelope? Kate couldn't even imagine, but at night when she tried to sleep, the possibilities kept her awake. She'd read enough Rex Stout and Agatha Christie novels to suspect—no, to be *positive*—that it hadn't contained an apology note to Mrs. Provakov's sister. Unless Ethel Rosenberg was Sophie's aunt.

Kate, reading every word and studying every photograph in the newspapers, now all predicting Mrs. Rosenberg's arrest, probably knew the Rosenbergs' relatives better than they did. Sophie's mother wasn't among them. Not Ethel's sister, not even a kissing cousin. And the woman in the Russian Tea Room's bathroom mirror had been Ethel Rosenberg.

Why would Mr. Provakov have lied to her? Could she

have passed a secret to a spy? Or had she just seen too many spy movies?

She'd thrown up in the middle of the night. This morning her mother wanted her to go see Dr. Einhorn, who lived right across the street. Kate thought she should be going to see Father Cunningham in the confessional, but didn't know what—if any—sin she'd committed. Still, she felt guilty. Maybe she could just talk to the priest. Or maybe not.

Could passing information, even without knowing that she had, get her in trouble with the FBI? Priests can never reveal what they hear in confession, but if she confessed nothing, just discussed her suspicions, would Father Cunningham feel obligated to turn her in?

Sophie seemed to have vanished. Or, at least, she hadn't returned Kate's phone calls. Three days had passed without even a thank-you for the cross.

"I hope you're not coming down with a stomach flu," her mother said, coming through Kate's bedroom door carrying a tray that held a tall glass of pink stuff. A really ugly shade of pink.

"What is that?" Kate had already made up her mind she wasn't going to drink it.

"Pepto-Bismol. Your father swears by it." Her mother lifted the glass. "Here, down it fast. You'll feel much better."

"I'd rather die."

"Don't be so silly, sweetheart. Be a good girl. If you swallow quickly, you won't even taste it."

"Just leave the glass on the nightstand, Mom. I want to go to the bathroom first. " And dump that god-awful mess down the toilet. Just like she'd gotten rid of the peas.

"This is not a vegetable, Kate. It's medicine. And I'm not leaving until you drink every drop."

A standoff. Kate, surprised that her mother had known about the flushed peas, caved first. The ugly pink stuff tasted worse than she'd expected, but fifteen minutes later, when Marlene arrived, her stomach had calmed down.

"Jeepers, Kate, you can't be sick; not when your father's taking us to dinner at the Park Sheraton." Marlene laid her garment bag at the foot of Kate's bed. "I brought over two outfits to model. You can tell me which one I should wear."

Wallowing in guilt, she'd forgotten all about tonight. Her father had invited Marlene and her parents to dinner at the hotel, then a visit to the famous Mermaid Lounge to hear Cy Coleman. Daddy, who played piano himself, was a big fan of Cy's.

"Get out of bed, Kate," Marlene ordered. "I'll polish your nails."

Feeling better than she had in days, Kate obeyed. "Toes, too? I just bought a brand-new bottle of Cherries in the Snow."

Kate's mother poked her head in. "Come on, girls. Scrambled eggs and English muffins are on the table. And we'll have a nice cup of tea."

Smiling as Marlene doused her eggs in ketchup, Kate was almost enjoying herself.

"So, Mrs. Norton, what are you wearing tonight?" Marlene's gold-flecked eyes sparkled.

"Well, I have two choices." Maggie Norton sighed.

"We'll have a fashion show and vote for our favorites," Marlene said. "My mother's out buying a dress right now. Said she didn't have a thing to wear."

They all laughed, knowing that Barbara Friedman had two closets and half of her husband's filled with pretty clothes.

"Did Mr. Norton meet Cy Coleman at the Mermaid Lounge?" Marlene asked Kate's mother. "It's neat to know a celebrity."

"I really shouldn't have another half," Kate's mother said, reaching for one. "The waist on my blue silk dress is a little snug already." She spread a tiny dab of strawberry jam across the muffin. "Let's see. I think Bill first met Mr. Coleman in the Park Sheraton's barbershop. It's in the basement, you know. Albert Anastasia is a client, too."

"The gangster?" Marlene looked impressed. "Gee, Mr. Norton's getting his hair cut with some interesting people."

"Well, Bill's office is only a couple of blocks away on Fifth Avenue," Maggie said, sounding proud. "And he does enjoy having a cocktail and listening to the music in the Mermaid Lounge, especially now that he's friendly with Cy."

Kate figured her father, who always enjoyed a drink, would have been stopping at the bar, celebrating his haircut, even without the piano player.

"Okay, girls, let's clear the table. And try on our dresses. Etta's off having a perm. She should be back in an hour or so. Then at four-thirty we're taking a taxi into the city with your parents, Marlene. Bill will meet us in the lobby."

"Is it a special occasion, Mrs. Norton?" Marlene drained her tea. "My mother wondered."

"Yes, Kate's father has just been promoted to division manager."

Kate wondered if she could get a new bike. A division manager, who had his hair cut with celebrities, ought to be able to afford a red Schwinn for his daughter.

Her father met them in front of the Mermaid Lounge. "I

thought we'd have cocktails here." He kissed his mother, his wife, then Kate, then Mrs. Friedman, and, finally, Marlene. Mr. Friedman put out his hand, "Congratulations, Bill."

The long mahogany bar, lined with leather stools, faced a couple of huge glass containers holding exotic fish and one beautiful mermaid. Most of the patrons were men. Kate stared at the mermaid, fascinated. How could she hold her breath for so long? Then Kate spotted a narrow tube spiraling upward from the girl's mouth.

Soft piano music filled the smoky room. Cy Coleman waved at Kate's father. She felt very special and didn't even groan when her father ordered Shirley Temples for her and Marlene.

"Could I see the barbershop, Mr. Norton?" Marlene asked. "I hear that Albert Anastasia gets his hair cut there."

Her father put down his scotch old-fashioned. "Sure, I'll take you and Kate on a little tour." He turned toward the four grown-ups. "We'll be back soon."

They walked across the lobby—not as grand as the Waldorf Astoria's or the Plaza's, but far nicer than the Biltmore's or the Roosevelt's. Kate and her mother had visited and rated the ladies' rooms in at least fifteen different hotels. With the exception of Saks Fifth Avenue, hotels had much more elegant bathrooms than department stores.

"Someday, Kate, we'll have your wedding reception here, in the rooftop ballroom."

Her father was always talking about the future: high school graduation, college, now a wedding. Kate hated to plan ahead. All she wanted was a red bike.

The Park Sheraton's barbershop was tucked away in a

narrow corridor of the basement. Nothing fancy. Jackson Heights had more attractive barbershops.

Marlene had her nose pressed up against the window, no doubt hoping to spot either a celebrity or a crook. But there were only two customers. And one had his face covered with a towel.

Kate stared at the tall, skinny man, standing with his back to the door. He turned and she gasped. It was the guy who worked with Mrs. Provakov. Her friend.

"What's the matter, Kate?" Her father asked.

"Nothing. I . . . er, nothing. I guess I thought the shop would be bigger."

The barber removed the towel from the seated man's face. This time, perhaps better prepared, Kate hid her shock. The man in the chair was Sophie's father.

Thirty

The Present

"If we can find out who made that phone call to Detective Parker while he was interviewing you, we've found the killer." Marlene spoke around a bite of bagel. Not Einstein's—almost as good as New York's—but frozen Arnold's bagels, toasted and spread with cream cheese, but light-years away from coming close to the real thing.

Kate had spent a restless night debating, among other things, if she should reveal S. J. Corbin's true identity to Marlene today or wait until after she'd confronted Sophie alone. Still jarred, she leaned toward the latter, though she wasn't sure why.

While it was true Parker had abruptly ended his interrogation about Kate's activities during the summer of 1950 after taking the mysterious call, the even bigger mystery was who'd told Parker to ask her about that summer in the first place. Only one person could have: S. J. Corbin, aka Sophie Provakov, her old friend. But why would Sophie have done that? Oh, God. Kate had to talk to Sophie before she told Marlene. Before she told anyone.

Ballou, who'd been walked and fed an hour ago, begged shamelessly at Marlene's knee. She slipped him a piece of bagel.

"I saw that, Marlene."

"Don't be such a curmudgeon. Now listen, I have a plan and we don't have much time. A hurricane's headed our way and we're going to be evacuated . . . again."

Murmuring endearments, Marlene picked Ballou up—with effort, Kate noted—and settled him on her lap. Thanks to his Aunt Marlene, the Westie was putting on weight.

"Okay, what's the plan?" Kate glanced at her watch. Fifteen minutes till the board meeting. She poured another cup of tea.

"We're going to pull off a Watergate-style break-in right here in our own condo. Well, actually, you are. I'm going to aid and abet, but not on the premises."

Kate almost dropped the teapot. "It's been coming for years, Marlene, but you're finally ready to be committed."

"Look, this may not even be against the law. How can it be breaking and entering if you have a key? As condo president, I have access to the keys to all the units. I'm turning one of them over to you." Marlene put Ballou back down on the kitchen floor, then stood, and reached into her bra. "Voila."

Kate shook her head. "No, way." Then, without intending to, asked, "Whose apartment?"

Marlene grinned. "Bob Seeley's, of course. He's our main man, isn't he?" She held the key in the open palm of her right hand. "He cooked the books, not only Weatherwise's, but Rosie's mob boyfriend's, too. He's a former Ranger, experienced in martial arts. You overheard Bob having a fight with Walt on the night before he was murdered. And Bob lied about being in bed. He could have stabbed Lee Parker, gotten rid of his bloody clothes, and changed into those crisply pressed pajamas."

Kate clasped her hands together as if in prayer, afraid she might reach out and grab the key. "Not that we're going to, but if we were, how would we pull it off? What if we got caught in the act?" She turned her two index fingers into a steeple. "Let me amend that: What if *I* got caught? I'd be breaking in alone, wouldn't I? You'd be at the meeting, right?"

"You won't be breaking in, Kate, you'll be *entering*. And, yes, alone. But don't worry, I'll be covering your back. I'll keep the meeting going until you finish your search and join us."

"And what, exactly, would I be looking for in Bob's apartment?"

"Where the old man keeps his medals."

"You really are crazy, Marlene." Kate stood, and Ballou, ever hopeful, headed toward his leash.

"No, I'm on target. Fussy old Bob would store all his important stuff together, not like me. My treasures are strewn about."

"An understatement." Her sister-in-law thrived on chaos. After a long search, Kate had once located Marlene's favorite black cocktail dress in the kitchen broom closet.

"We can't all be June Cleaver. But you think neat, and that's why you're perfect for this job." Marlene smiled. "Just like you, I'll bet he has all his important papers, like family birth and death certificates, passport, canceled checks, old income tax forms, army discharge—and yes, his medals—plus whatever stuff he has on Weatherwise, in one location. A file cabinet. Or in folders in his desk drawers. Or on a shelf in a closet."

"If he stowed everything in a safe, we're sunk." Kate grabbed a paper towel and wiped her damp forehead, realizing she'd just committed to breaking into—no, to *entering*—Bob's apartment.

"Well, then we move on to Plan B." Marlene whipped out her compact and lipstick.

"Which is?" Kate, reaching around Ballou, rummaged under the sink for her plastic gloves. Wouldn't want to leave any fingerprints, would she?

"I'm working on it." Marlene appraised herself in the dining room mirror, gave Ballou a pat on the back, kissed Kate on the cheek, then checked her watch. "It's nine-fifty-five. Be in the rec room by ten-fifteen. I can't make a one-item meeting last forever. No matter what happens, don't stay in Bob's apartment any longer than fifteen minutes."

Thirty·one

Not wanting to be spotted on the elevator, Kate dashed to the enclosed stairwell and climbed up to the seventh floor. No one in Ocean Vista, except for Rosie, ever used the stairs. She'd never been in Bob's apartment—in the same tier, but four floors above hers, his balcony would have an even better view.

Panting hard, she pushed open the door into the corridor that led to Bob's unit. If anyone spotted her here, she'd have to abort the mission.

Children's laughter stopped her cold. Kids were seldom seen, never mind heard, in Ocean Vista's hallways. Oh God, yes. Lydia Rosen's two grandsons were visiting from Cleveland.

Lydia probably hadn't gone to the meeting, had stayed home with the boys. Maybe to take them to the pool. Or maybe to get ready to evacuate. If they left the apartment within the next sixty seconds, Kate would be caught in the act.

The act of what? Was she committing a crime or wasn't she? Still undecided, she pulled Bob's spare key out of her pocket and, with a shaky hand, inserted it into the lock.

The living room was as sterile and as spare as Marlene had imagined. A ubiquitous South Florida off-white couch, this one structured, severe. Square, modern tables. Firm, narrow club chairs, designed exclusively for people with bottoms as skinny as Bob's. Not a pillow in sight. Not a stray piece of paper anywhere. Not an opened book on a table. And no bookcases. No magazines. No newspapers. Didn't he read? White plantation shutters covered the balcony door, keeping out the sunlight and blocking the ocean view.

Okay, where would the old man keep his medals? She'd start in the master bedroom.

The books were in the bedroom. Except for the public library, she'd never seen so many books in one place. Biographies, novels (including a complete set of Dickens), Roman history, nonfiction (heavy on the paranormal), financial planning guides, lots of erotica, and two shelves of bibles, ranging from the King James version to the Latin vulgate to the Book of Mormon, filled nine bookcases, covering three walls.

An art deco bed, was centered in the wall opposite the door. Framed black-and-white photographs of Fred Astaire and Ginger Rogers dancing were displayed above the walnut headboard.

A tall armoire, also art deco, with double doors, stood to the right of the bed.

She had no doubt the armoire would be where the old

man kept his medals. And with any luck, as Marlene had predicted, everything else that mattered to him.

Adjusting her plastic gloves, she darted across the room and opened the double doors. Three wide, deep wooden drawers held neatly labeled file folders, about twenty to a drawer. Bob Seeley had used black ink to print big, block letters identifying each folder's contents on its upper right-hand corner. She knelt in front of the bottom drawer, reached straight back to the W's, and pulled Walt Weatherwise's file. Her knee cracked as she stood up.

The folder held a standard, business-size white envelope. If she ripped it open, Bob would know that someone had been in the apartment. It wasn't sealed all the way to the corners. Maybe she could pry open the flap, then reseal it. She used her pinkie to gently prod. Bit by bit, the flap lifted. Hooray! The envelope held a single sheet of folded paper. A key fell out, landing on the white tiled floor, clanging louder than a church bell. The paper was blank. The key would open a safe deposit box in a Sun Trust Bank in Oakland Park. Damn. Damn. Damn.

Could there be something else? Where should she look? Which file should she start with?

Kate fought a strong urge to dump all the folders on the floor. Make a mess. Make Bob mad as hell. Then, in the front of the second drawer, she spotted a file with five red stars highlighting a label that read: KIRK ISLAND.

Oh God, help me. She sank back down on her knees.

So it had come to this: Her past flying out of the dark, unexamined corner of her mind, and blindsiding her. Had she somehow known all along? She'd suspected, then rejected, a Long Island connection, hadn't she? One of the Kirk Island children now grown old? Or Sophie herself?

She stood, shaking, her fingers sweating in the plastic gloves. She lifted the folder, opened it, and, feeling guilty and ashamed, rifled through it.

A photograph of a smiling boy, about six or seven, wearing a suit with short pants, standing between a tall, handsome man and a pretty, dark-haired young woman. An inscription on the back read, EASTER SUNDAY, KIRK ISLAND, 1944. A marriage certificate for Ruth Ann Evans, 22, and Robert Matthew Seeley, 24, dated June 1937. A deed to a house on Kirk Island, dated November 18, 1937. A birth certificate for Robert Matthew Seeley, Jr., dated May 2, 1938, place of birth, Kirk Island, New York. A death certificate for Ruth Ann Seeley, 35, dated August 18, 1950, place of death, Kirk Island, New York. A death certificate for Robert Matthew Seeley, 37, dated August 18, 1950, place of death, Kirk Island, New York.

Bob would have been twelve when his parents died. She reached into her shirt pocket for a tissue.

Moments passed. She stood, inert, unable to move, the folder frozen in her hand.

She sensed rather than heard someone else in the apartment. She couldn't move. Behind her, she heard footsteps on the tile.

"Turn around, Kate."

She pivoted and faced S. J. Corbin. Her old friend, Sophie.

Kate sighed. Nothing mattered now, did it? "Until last night, I'd never seen you wear that cross, Sophie."

"I've worn it often, Kate, over the last half century. These past couple of days, I've been wondering how long it would take you to recognize me. I guess I've changed more than I thought. But I hoped the cross might give you a clue to my identity."

"Playing mind games, Sophie? Like your father. He was always good at them."

"Oh, Kate." Sophie shook her head, then put on her glasses, came closer, and pointed to the folder. "Kirk Island. So you've found the motive, haven't you?"

Thirty·two

Thursday, August 10, 1950

"Your friend Sophie's father is a strange one, Katie." Her father sliced the roast beef. "Rare?" Blood ran from the meat to the platter.

"He's okay, Daddy." Kate sounded defensive. Though she wouldn't admit it to her parents, she herself believed Mr. Provakov's behavior went way beyond strange.

"Not mutually exclusive." Her father shrugged.

Kate wasn't sure what he meant by that, so she waited.

"Pink," her mother said, pointing to Kate's plate. "She doesn't like it too bloody."

Her father sliced a piece from the roast's narrow end. "Will this do?"

"Perfect." Kate smiled. "Thanks."

"Drinking a glass of blood would do the girl good, Maggie."

"I'm not a vampire, Daddy."

"You used to love to down the red juices when you were a little girl, Katie."

It might be better to discuss Sophie's father's strange ways than to get into a blood-drinking debate with her own father, who, a little strange himself, was also into health food, like yogurt and wheat germ. "What were you saying about Mr. Provakov?"

"Well Provakov pretended he didn't recognize you in the Park Sheraton's barbershop last week, then got all flustered when you waved and introduced him to me and Marlene." Her father placed the meat next to Kate's mashed potatoes. "This evening I ran into him on Roosevelt Avenue, coming out of Brady's, and he acted like he'd never met me."

"Then what happened, Daddy?" Kate felt nervous, and with good cause. She hadn't told her parents about her encounter with Ethel Rosenberg in the Russian Tea Room and she hadn't gone to confession, though she worried about having committed, at the very least, a serious sin of omission.

"Nothing. I said hello, then when he ignored me, I just moved on," her father said, then turned his attention to his dinner. "Very good, Maggie."

Her father would have found Mr. Provakov's behavior even weirder if he'd been aware that the skinny young man who'd been in the barbershop had visited the Provakov's apartment, that the two men had only pretended not to know each other. Complicating things further, Mr. Provakov had no clue that Kate and Sophie had been watching when Sophie's mother had brought her coworker home.

Worse, Kate hadn't told either her parents or her grandmother that Sophie hadn't spoken to her since the birthday lunch at the Russian Tea Room.

Last week at the hotel, Mr. Provakov told Kate that Sophie had gone to Cleveland to visit a distant cousin. Why hadn't Sophie returned Kate's calls before she left? She'd left three different messages with Mr. Provakov. But Sophie never called to say good-bye. Or to thank Kate for her birthday present. Something was wrong. Very wrong.

She'd reread the last chapter of *Little Women* for the four-teenth time before she fell asleep. Kate hadn't wanted to let go of Jo and Amy; however, the formerly beloved book had become her secret vice since she'd moved on to more grown-up heroines like Scarlett and Natasha.

Secrets, even literary secrets, were dangerous.

She tossed and turned between three fast-paced, terror-filled book-based nightmares. In the last one, Kate, dressed in a hoop skirt like Jo March's, and blindfolded, was about to be shot to death by a Union Army firing squad for treason. She'd passed a note, containing Sherman's battle plan, to one of Lee's men.

"Ready." A guttural voice ordered. "Aim." She could hear the rifles being cocked. "Fire!"

She woke up in a sweat, saying, "I swear I didn't know what was in the note."

Her bedside clock read eleven-thirty-five. She'd been in bed for two hours. And she'd only clicked off her bed-side lamp at eleven.

Her hair and her pillow were soaked. She couldn't catch her breath. Gulping, she willed herself to calm down, to tame her runaway heartbeat, and to stay awake. She didn't dare fall back to sleep.

Thirty·three

Friday, August 11, 1950

Even sinners sleep, Kate thought as her alarm went off. She'd last glanced at the clock at three A.M. It was now seven thirty.

Weary—maybe total exhaustion would be her eternal punishment—she struggled out of bed and made her way to the bathroom.

Of all things, she had to go to a nine A.M. funeral mass with her mother. A neighbor, not a friend. So Mom wouldn't be joining the funeral procession following the hearse to Calvary after church. They hardly knew old Mrs. Porter, but Kate's mother seemed to thrive on burials. She enjoyed throwing a rose on top of the casket right before the gravediggers covered it with dirt. Kate considered herself lucky to be spared this one. She had a date with Marlene to see *Father of the Bride* this afternoon.

After the requiem mass, Kate and her mother dissected the service over a second breakfast at Wolke's, then parted ways. Maggie had errands to run and Kate had money to burn. Etta had given her five dollars. "For no reason, just because." Her grandmother did that every couple of months. Kate planned to buy a book at Miss Ida's. She'd treat Marlene to White Castle hamburgers and an orange crush with the change.

Kate, Miss Ida's only customer, browsed. Rex Stout had a new mystery. The entire Norton family loved Nero Wolfe and Archie. Or maybe she'd get Perry Mason's latest case. She ran her hand across a pile of recently arrived paperback mysteries, admiring how smooth and fresh their covers felt, and inhaling the scent of cologne. The proprietor smelled like one of Wolfe's orchids.

How she loved the bookstore. So quiet. So full of promise.

"Hello, stranger." Sophie. She'd recognize that voice anywhere.

Starting, Kate sent several books flying off the counter as she spun around. "I thought you were away." She sounded tense, but not upset, though she was. "In Cleveland."

"Well, outside Cleveland. In some dreary town, smaller than Jackson Heights. With only one movie theater. Nothing to do. And my batty old Russian cousin's so cheap she wouldn't allow me to make a long distance call."

Did that mean Sophie would have called if she could? Kate hoped—no, prayed—that was true. "I left a couple messages with your father."

"He only phoned one time, but he mentioned you'd asked for me. He should have given you my number."

Sophie looked puzzled. Worried. "Papa has a lot on his mind."

"Yes, I think he does." Kate also thought Mr. Provakov had used her. But for what purpose? "He's been acting odd."

"It's good to see you, Kate. What are you doing this afternoon?" Sophie, ignoring Kate's comment, seemed to have gotten over her concern for her father. "Can we go to the movies? *Father of the Bride* is playing at the Boulevard."

Not even thinking about asking Marlene first, Kate said, "Yes." And she didn't question Sophie about her "aunt" in the Russian Tea Room's bathroom. There'd be time for that later.

"The Boulevard's always freezing. I'd like to stop home first and get a sweater. Is that okay?"

"Sure. I'll go with you. I'm meeting up with Marlene at the White Castle at twelve-thirty; we're going to bring a couple of bags of hamburgers to the movies."

"Good," Sophie said. "We'll have lunch at the matinee. I like that."

Five well-dressed, middle-aged matrons came into the store. The one in the feathered hat said, "Good morning, Miss Ida. We need five copies of all of F. Scott Fitzgerald's novels. We're starting a book group."

Miss Ida smiled. The store's morning sales had moved from slow to profitable.

"I'll take the Nero Wolfe. And I know Mom will be in for the new Perry Mason." She put her five-dollar bill on the counter, letting the ladies see Miss Ida had other good customers.

Sophie and Kate walked the five blocks, chatting as if they'd never been apart. Strange how much Kate's mood had improved, how delighted she was to be Sophie's friend again. Yet, she had some doubts. Sophie's lack of laughter. Intense, Kate's mother had said. And she wouldn't drop Marlene. Her forever best friend. They'd just gotten back on track. A trio of friends might prove complicated, but this morning, with the sun warming her face and a slight breeze blowing through her hair, Kate felt nothing less than pure joy.

"The carnival's opening tonight." Sophie pointed to the vacant lot directly across Thirty-fourth Avenue from her apartment house. Workers were putting up poker booths and cotton candy and hot dog stands. Minus any riders, the Tilt-a-Whirl and Ferris wheel were going through test runs.

Kate had never missed a carnival. "I'll be there around seven with Marlene and my parents. Are you coming?"

"Papa says the carnival is decadent." Sophie shrugged. "I don't know if he'll let me go."

Kate, not sure what *decadent* meant, said nothing.

Sophie used her own key to get into the lobby. "I think my father went to a meeting." Kate didn't have a key to her house. Either her mother or her grandmother was always home. And if for some reason they weren't, Mrs. Friedman had a spare key. Kate hadn't resented that arrangement until now.

The elevator still reeked of cabbage. Kate imagined that, decades from now, the building would smell the same. Smells, like sins, weren't easily removed.

With a smaller key, Sophie opened the door to the apartment. Standing in the small foyer, Kate could hear voices coming from the living room.

"Oh," Sophie said, "I didn't think anyone would be here." She sounded upset. Almost frightened.

Kate followed her into the living room. Mr. and Mrs. Provakov, and the tall, skinny blond man were huddled over what appeared to be a chart or a map.

Mr. Provakov looked up, then snatched the chart out of the younger man's hand and muttered something in Russian to Sophie, who flushed deep red.

Half-filled cartons were scattered around the room. Could they be moving?

The seldom-seen Irina Provakov looked over at Kate. "This is Sophie's friend, Kate Kennedy." Mrs. Provakov spoke in accented English, her voice low. Almost monotone. She gestured toward the skinny guy. "This is my colleague, Mr. Wager."

"We work together at the Weather Bureau," Mr. Wager said.

Her husband frowned, then spat out harsh, rapid Russian. Kate felt sure Sophie's father was cursing. The young man had just said that Irina Provakov worked at the Weather Bureau. Could Mr. Provakov be angry because he hadn't wanted Kate to know where his wife worked? But why would that matter?

The young man stared at a carpet on the wall, mumbling, "Pleased to meet you, Kate."

She felt relieved because the gangly Mr. Wager sounded a lot like Henry Fonda.

Sophie ran into the bedroom and returned with her sweater. "Let's get out of here, Kate."

Mr. Provakov, usually so strict, never even questioned where they were going. Neither did Sophie's mother.

"What's wrong?" Kate asked the quiet Sophie, as they walked over to Northern Boulevard, heading down to the White Castle.

Sophie shook her head. "I can't talk about it, Kate. Let's just enjoy the afternoon."

Though Marlene shot a quizzical glance at Kate, she acted pleased to see Sophie, and her ceaseless chatter made the six blocks to the movie bearable.

Kate had no way of knowing *Father of the Bride* would be the last movie she'd ever see with Sophie.

No way of knowing the Provakov family would be gone by morning.

No way of knowing Ethel Rosenberg had been arrested today.

No way of knowing one week from today, on August 18, 1950, the United States would be struck with a nuclear *accident* set in motion this afternoon in Sophie's living room.

Thirty·four

The Present

"Kirk Island?" The site of the nuclear disaster was the motive for Weatherwise's murder? Bob Seeley's parents died that day. And what had brought Sophie Provakov to Ocean Vista? A motive of her own? Kate wanted to collapse on the bed, gather her thoughts, make some sense out of this. She wished she had a Pepcid AC.

"Put the file back, Kate. We have to get out of here." Sophie glanced over her shoulder at the bedroom door.

As surely as if a switch had been pulled, a light went on in the dark, never unexamined corner of Kate's brain. "That young guy who'd worked with your mother . . . he disappeared in 1950, then became Uncle Weatherwise, didn't he?"

Sophie nodded. "Yes. Get rid of that folder. Now!"

Had Kate recognized anything about Weatherwise?

After all, she'd changed. Marlene had changed. And she hadn't even recognized Sophie.

More than fifty-five years had passed. Anyone who'd survived that long had changed. The blond, gangly man had grown fat and bald. And old—the best disguise of all. Had morphed into the odious Uncle Weatherwise. She should have known. Maybe she'd been lying to herself. It wouldn't be the first time.

"Damn it, Kate, pull yourself together."

A door slammed shut. Footsteps clicked on the tile in the hall. Someone was marching toward the bedroom.

Kate jumped off the bed, stuck the folder back, closed the armoire, and yanked off her plastic gloves, sticking them in her pocket. She wanted to wipe the know-it-all grin off Sophie's face.

"Let me do the talking, Kate." Sophie smoothed her skirt. "Get over to the window. Pull open the shutter. Pretend you're admiring the view."

"What the hell?" Bob Seeley shouted. Very out of character, Kate thought. But then, so was cooking the books, stealing your clients' money, and, possibly, having murdered a weatherman and a detective. "What are you doing here, Kate?"

Entering, but not breaking in. No, that wouldn't cut it. She stared out the window in silence.

"Ms. Corbin, I thought you were assessing my unit's market value." Seeley sounded frustrated, angry. Like Weatherwise felt before he'd been murdered? And was Bob planning on selling his condo? Moving?

"Please relax, Mr. Seeley, I'm doing my job, acting on your behalf." Sophie had assumed her S. J. Corbin persona.

"Why is this woman here? I trusted you with my key,

Ms. Corbin. This is an outrage." His voice cracked. "Kate and her pal, Marlene, were nosing around Miami yesterday, interrogating my former coworkers."

The blonde receptionist had to be the tattletale. Mr. Moose wouldn't have blown off two new investors.

"I pride myself on being the eyes and the ears of my clients. This morning, I ran into Mrs. Kennedy on her way to the condo meeting and, just by chance, she mentioned how much she loved Ocean Vista and her apartment, but really wished she could be on a higher floor. Knowing she lived in your tier, I couldn't let that golden opportunity slip by." S.J. sighed. "Just think, Mr. Seeley, I might have appraised your unit and sold it during my first visit."

Damn, S.J. was good. Knowing the Realtor was lying through her beautifully capped teeth, Kate almost believed her.

"Of course, if I'd been aware that Mrs. Kennedy had invaded your former office, or in any way violated your trust, I would never have shown her your apartment."

Seeley, seemingly stumped, stared at S.J.

Kate figured the next line was hers. "I've decided I prefer the third floor."

S.J. smiled. "Nothing ventured."

"I would have had to spend a bundle to put some sizzle in this place. So, thanks for the tour, but no thanks S.J." Kate turned from the window, and crossed in front of Bob on her way to the bedroom door. She paused, meeting his eyes. "Did I miss anything important at the meeting?"

He blinked first. "Yes, we're under mandatory evacuation this evening. Igor has been upgraded to a Category Four hurricane. It's expected to hit Fort Lauderdale late tomorrow."

"Then I better start packing." Kate stepped into the

hall, then pulled a Columbo, sticking her head back into the room. "When did you decide to move out of Ocean Vista, Bob? Before or after Weatherwise was murdered?" She didn't wait for his answer.

"Where the hell have you been?" Marlene shouted, running from the kitchen to the foyer, when Kate arrived back home. "Bob left the meeting at least ten minutes ago. What happened? Did he catch you in the act? Should I call F. Lee Bailey?"

Ballou, on Marlene's heels, cocked his head at his mistress. The Westie wanted in on whatever was going on.

"No, I don't need an attorney, but I could use a cup of tea. Just let me put the kettle on."

"I tried to keep the meeting going, but we had the TV on, then the governor ordered an evacuation from Miami to Palm Beach. There was nothing more to say. I'll make you a cup of tea, but *I* need a martini."

"It's not even eleven o'clock, Marlene."

"Somewhere the sun is over the yardarm; I'll use my imagination."

"Your imagination almost landed me in jail."

Thirty minutes later, a tepid wave in a smooth sea washed over Kate's toes. The calm before the storm, she supposed. Uncle Weatherwise's replacement had made Igor sound as wicked as Katrina; she'd turned off the television. She had enough turmoil in her life without listening to dire predictions.

Kate couldn't decide whose behavior was worse,

Marlene's or Ballou's. Both wanted their own way and both were demanding Kate's full attention

The Westie wouldn't budge, engrossed in investigating a dead crab, using the shell like a hockey puck. Her sister-in-law wouldn't shut up, rehashing and analyzing every word of Kate's abridged tale of the break-in and its aftermath. Kate hadn't mentioned the Kirk Island connection. She couldn't. Not until she had a chance to question Sophie.

When Marlene had gone home to change, Kate left two messages on S. J. Corbin's answering machine and alerted Miss Mitford to keep an eye out for the Realtor.

Sophie had proved to be a smooth liar. Had she always been one or had she developed that skill after becoming a broker?

"So where did Sophie go?" Marlene, as relentless as a federal prosecutor, wouldn't quit. "She and her parents just vanished, right? And you never heard from her again."

"For God's sake, Bob came home; we had no time to play catch up."

"Yo!" Coming from behind, Rosie O'Grady's greeting could probably be heard in Cuba. Or at least in Bimini. Kate couldn't remember when she'd been so glad to be interrupted.

"Why ain't you two packing? We gotta go tonight. The governor or FEMA or some idiot decided we can't take our own cars." She laughed. "Mine's in police custody, anyway. The first bus arrives at six."

"You're right, Rosie," Kate said. "Come on, Ballou, we're heading home."

"Are you two old enough to remember that hurricane back in 1946, I think? Knocked down a lotta trees in the boroughs. And wacked the hell out of eastern Long Island.

I was staying on Kirk Island at my boyfriend's." Rosie pushed her hair off her face. The breeze had picked up. "The wind howled all evening. Blew the roof off his bungalow. The whole island got flooded. We climbed out an attic window. Thought we'd be dead by dawn, but a fishing boat rescued us."

Kirk Island. Could Kate be going crazy? She fought panic, tried to breathe deeply, but the past seemed to have popped up and grabbed her by the throat, choking her.

"That nuclear thing, later, in 1950, wasn't that on Kirk Island, too?" Marlene asked.

"Yeah," Rosie said. "Friday, August eighteenth. I'll never forget. Lucky I was dancing onstage at Radio City. Paul, my boyfriend—well, we were engaged by then—died that day."

Thirty·five

"Mom," Kevin said, "Don't forget to take all your financial information, and your credit cards, check book, and what else, hon?"

"Income tax forms for the last three years." Kate could hear her daughter-in-law shouting instructions. She pictured Jennifer's smooth blonde hair close to Kevin's wiry, graying, auburn curls. "Charlie's pension info. Your Social Security and Medicare cards, plus any supplemental medical insurance cards. And all the cash in the condo. If the power goes, Kate, you won't be able to use an ATM."

"Did you get that, Mom?"

She sighed. "Jennifer makes it sound as if I won't be coming home again." When had she started to think of Ocean Vista as home?

"Igor may become a Category Five, Mom. And it may hit sooner than expected." She could hear the concern in

Kevin's voice. "You may not be going home, at least not for a very long time. Peter's on the phone with Aunt Marlene now, telling her what to bring."

"Kevin, your Aunt Marlene couldn't find those records if her life depended on it." Oh God. Marlene's future might depend on finding them. "Sorry, poor attempt at humor. I'll go down and help her as soon as I get my act together. Please don't worry, darling, we'll be fine. Kiss the girls and Jennifer for me."

Kevin and Peter, her Irish twins, born a year apart. How Charlie had loved them.

"I love you, Mom."

"And I love all of you." She hung up as the first tear fell.

"Focus, Kate," she said aloud, knowing she couldn't. Kirk Island kept getting in the way. Damn.

Yet another motive from fifty-six years ago. Rosie O'Grady had lost her lover in the nuclear disaster. And Bob Seeley had lost his parents. It couldn't be coincidental that Rosie, Bob, and Walt had all wound up living at Ocean Vista. That Weatherwise had been Bob's client. That Bob had stolen the weatherman's money. That Bob had convinced Walt to move up here from Miami. That Uncle Weatherwise had been the young man she'd met in Sophie Provakov's apartment on the day that Ethel Rosenberg had been arrested.

She sobbed as she opened the medicine cabinet, unable to decide what to pack. Or what to tell Marlene.

Rosie had chattered all the way back to the condo, seeming—or pretending—not to realize that she'd dropped a bombshell. Again, all those decades of shared body language had paid off. Kate's raised left eyebrow kept Marlene at bay.

Kate had said a quick good-bye to Rosie and Marlene, promising to call her sister-in-law. Since Peter was more chatty than Kevin, Marlene and he were probably still on the phone, but Kate's reprieve wouldn't last long.

A loud rap on the front door startled Kate. Ballou, at her feet, yapped. She dropped the Listerine bottle in the sink. The glass shattered. The familiar medicinal smell seemed intoxicating, overpowering.

Together, Kate and the Westie ran through the foyer. She dreaded dealing with Marlene. Confronting the past. Facing the future.

She yanked the door open.

Mary Frances, beautifully groomed and dressed in a green designer sweatsuit that matched her eyes, stood in the corridor. She cuddled an uncannily lifelike baby doll, wearing a pink romper and matching bonnet.

She stepped into the foyer. "I'm not going, Kate. I can't leave my girls behind. Please take Emma with you. She'll fit in somewhere." The former nun sounded calm. Too calm.

"Listen to me, Mary Frances." Kate aimed for June Cleaver, but came across more like Murphy Brown. "Ocean Vista and your dolls will survive this hurricane. And you're not staying home alone. If you don't evacuate, I'll be forced to stay with you. So go upstairs and finish packing."

"I can't." Mary Frances cried, clutching the doll to her chest.

The Westie, who'd never cottoned to Mary Frances, rubbed his nose against her ankle.

"See, Ballou wants you to come, too."

"But . . ."

"Look, give me Emma. I'll put her in my briefcase. It's

expandable." She'd leave the income tax forms behind. If all went well, Jennifer would never have to know. "And bring Jackie O and Marilyn. Wrap them in a blanket. We'll fit them into our bags somehow."

"You really believe Ocean Vista won't be flooded? That my other dolls won't be blown away?"

"Absolutely," Kate lied.

"Okay. I'll call you when I'm ready. Can we leave on the same bus?"

"Sure." Kate, not having a clue how they'd board the busses, lied again. "Meet me in the lobby at five-thirty. If you don't, I'm sending Miss Mitford up to get you."

Mary Frances almost smiled.

Kate placed Emma on the bed, as gently as if she were a real baby, then returned to the bathroom, picked up the glass, and scrubbed the sink. Feeling somewhat better—needed?—she got serious about packing, her organizational skills, at least temporarily, trumping her fear. She even turned the TV on.

"A Four that may turn into a Category Five, picking up speed, heading for Palmetto Beach." Great. Ocean Vista would be ground zero. She prayed Mary Frances wasn't watching the young weatherman, who now seemed frightened enough to deliver the forecast straight. No editorializing. No histrionics. And so much more terrifying.

Ballou yelped. Then Kate heard the knocking, too.

"Okay, that must be Auntie Marlene."

Again, they hurried to the front door. Kate flung it open.

S. J. Corbin said, "May I come in, Kate?"

Though she'd been tracking Sophie down, leaving her messages, wanting to talk to her, Kate had dreaded seeing her. And now she'd arrived, asking to come in.

"The living room's straight ahead." Kate, nervous, laughed. "But, of course, you know that. It's just like Bob's."

"Only lower." Sophie smiled, sitting on Kate's off-white couch, also very much like Bob's.

Kate sat in the club chair, facing her. Silent strangers, sharing a terrible secret from a lifetime ago. She couldn't go there yet. She'd begin with a more recent betrayal. "You told Detective Parker to ask me about the summer of 1950, didn't you, Sophie?"

Ballou stayed at Kate's side, his paw on her foot.

"Yes, I did. Anonymously. Weatherwise was murdered because of the Kirk Island nuclear explosion." Sophie bit her lip. "I needed to steer Parker in the right direction."

Kate didn't blink. Hadn't she been expecting this? She'd buried the past in a dark corner of her mind, but she couldn't cleanse the stain on her soul. "You were going to use me as your pawn?"

"Yes. I'm sorry, Kate. Exposing the past was necessary to reveal the killer."

"And did you phone Parker, again, while he was interviewing me?"

"No," Sophie sighed, "but the killer must have. To feed him some lies. To lure him to Rosie's car."

Exactly what Marlene had said: *If we find out who made the second phone call . . . we've found the killer.* "Sophie, do you know who murdered Uncle Weatherwise?"

"One motive: revenge. More than one suspect." Sophie shrugged. "I can't be certain."

Her almond-shaped brown eyes looked hurt. Confused. Kate felt the decades disappear. Evaporate. As if they were kids in Queens again.

"Where did you go, Sophie? Why didn't you ever call?"

"You know the answer to those questions, don't you? A smart girl like you. Such a newspaper reader."

Silent, Kate rubbed Ballou's neck.

"What could I have said, Kate? I still don't know what to say."

Thirty·six

January 18, 1957

Kate had a crush on a cute cop, Charlie Kennedy, a great job as an Eastern Airlines stewardess, and a 3.8 grade point average in her night classes at Hunter College. She couldn't remember ever having been so happy. Or feeling so full of promise.

Then, at cocktail hour, her father finished his old-fashioned, folded the *Journal-American* to the op-ed page, and handed it to her. "Read this, Katie. Drew Pearson's assistant, that young hot shot, Jack Anderson, fancies himself an investigative reporter. Seems he's scratched an itch about that explosion out on Kirk Island, back in 1950. Says the U.S. government has always called it a 'nuclear accident,' but Anderson's story reveals a long-planned, complicated espionage plot. And, guess what, my girl? You knew the spies."

KIRK ISLAND EXPOSED

In the early 1930s, a Russian, Boris Provakov, and his wife, Irina, were dispatched by the KGB to the US. Their mission: to establish a legitimate low-key lifestyle, then wait until called at some future date to serve the mother country. They were instructed to avoid political activity and any contact with the Bolshevik movement.

The Russian, trained as a draftsman, was adept at mechanical, electrical, and geographical drawings to precise specification. He held a series of jobs with construction companies and later established a consulting business enabling him to accept jobs on consignment and to work in his apartment. The wife held a series of clerical jobs. Their only daughter, Sophie, was born in 1937.

And had became Kate's friend in 1950. Terrified, she forced herself to read on.

In 1948, at the height of the cold war, Russia had achieved nuclear capability. The Berlin Wall and the Berlin airlift were both in place. Families, including immigrants, across the US sent CARE packages to Europe. Using a code established before the Provakovs' departure from Russia, an undercover KGB agent contacted Boris Provakov. His long-delayed mission: determine the wind-flow patterns along the East Coast and, using these, determine the precise location for a small nuclear detonation that would spread lethal radioactivity to fewer than one hundred people in a confined setting somewhere on the East Coast of the US.

In a rare breach of information compartmentalization, the KGB agent explained how the Russian navy planned a "nuclear accident" that would kill a small number" of US citizens. Russia hoped the resultant political pressure would force the US to accept Russian demands to stop the Berlin airlift and agree to a unilateral commitment to halt production of nuclear weapons.

Boris Provakov determined the best source for the vital wind current information would be the US Weather Bureau. Irina obtained a file clerk position in the Bureau's NYC office and by 1950 had become a valued and trusted employee, serving in the Atmospheric Research branch.

Irina made friends with Will Wager who'd grown up in the Midwest and was lonely in the big city. The weatherman accepted the friendship of the Russian family, loved the ethnic food, played chess with Boris, and became a frequent visitor at the Queens apartment.

Provekov told Will of his fascination with wind currents and how they affected weather, sea patterns, storms, and about one of his avocations: hot-air ballooning. The Russian shared Will's dream of taking a hot-air balloon to sea on a large boat, then floating back

*to shore in the balloon, even though the upper
atmosphere's prevailing winds would push it
in the opposite direction.*

    *Will, delighted to help, became a font of in-
formation. He brought reams of data about
the wind currents off the coast of Long Island
and how they varied by the season, and by
earth and sea temperature. He even assisted
Boris Provakov in plotting the currents on
Mercator map projections.*

    *By August of 1950, Provakov had the infor-
mation providing the desired solution: the
precise longitude and latitude to unleash a
small nuclear explosion where the wind currents would carry the radioactive cloud over
Kirk Island, originally a Dutch settlement, off
the coast of Long Island. He reached his KGB
contact who, under suspicion himself, advised
Provakov to use an unknown third party to
pass the data to Ethel Rosenberg.*

Oh dear God. She'd been the unwitting third party,
passing the note in the bathroom at the Russian Tea Room.

    *When the bomb exploded at sea off Kirk
Island, on August 18, 1950, five people died.
Two hundred and fifty others contracted radiation sickness. Fifty more people have died
over the last six years.*

    *The explosion didn't have the desired effect
on the American people; instead, stern
protests were given to the Russian government*

and the cold war was pursued with renewed vigor.

The Russian defector said Boris and Irina Provakov had slipped into Canada a week before the explosion, then returned to Russia. The defector had no idea where their only daughter, Sophie, had gone. She might have returned to Russia with her parents.

Kate, now sick with guilt, had been wondering what had happened to her friend for years.

What had happened to Will Wager was another story. When questioned by Anderson for his upcoming exposé, Wager realized he'd played a critical part in the death of U.S. citizens.

Betting he'd be exonerated, he made a dangerous move, confessing he'd been duped into giving critical weather data to Provakov, then offering to help the CIA with the investigation.

His bold move had paid off. With great fanfare, Anderson ended his article by praising Wager's patriotism.

Kate felt like a traitor.

Thirty·seven

The Present

"I need to know, Sophie. Did you go to Russia with your parents?" Kate gestured toward the couch. "Would you like some tea?"

"In a glass with a long silver spoon?" Sophie shook her head, then sat on the edge of the couch, appearing poised for flight. "No tea, thank you." With the palm of her hand, she brushed her short dark hair away from her forehead.

Not a gray strand. She must color it. Kate's thoughts meandered toward the mundane, maybe to postpone dealing with the truth.

"I didn't go to Russia, Kate. I never saw my parents again."

"Never?"

Sophie's face sagged. Her carefully applied makeup

seemed to highlight rather than conceal the deep lines running from her nose to her mouth.

"I'm convinced I was part of their cover. A child would have made them seem more like a normal family." She stood, then walked toward the glass doors. "The wind has picked up. A beach chair just flew into the pool."

"Your father loved you, Sophie."

"He used you. I think he used me, too." She turned around and stared at Kate, unblinking. "When I came home after seeing *Father of the Bride* that Friday after-noon, my parents were packed and ready to roll. They went to Canada. I was sent to Ohio to live with my mother's old cousin. The one I'd visited earlier that sum-mer."

"And your parents didn't call you before they left for Russia?"

"No." Sophie's eyes grew darker. "They never got in touch with the cousin either. God, how she resented me. I got the hell out of there at sixteen, called myself S.J. and waitressed my way through Kent State. A guidance counselor helped me get a partial scholarship."

Such a sad story. But was it true? "Then what?"

"I became a teacher in Cleveland, married a great guy, Mike Corbin. He and I traveled to the USSR in the mid-sixties to search for my parents, but they'd vanished. None of their relatives or old friends knew what had hap-pened to them. Or where they'd gone." She shrugged. "If they returned to the USSR, they lived far away from Moscow. Who knows? Maybe they never left Canada."

"Oh, Sophie."

"We never had any children. When Mike died, I moved down to Florida and became a Realtor. I've become very successful, Kate. Much of my money has been spent tracking down the victims of Kirk Island. Those who'd lost their parents in the nuclear explosion."

Kate heard the anger in Sophie's voice and thought about Bob Seeley's parents. Their smiling faces in the black-and-white photographs. Their death certificates. "Why?"

"I'd discovered that two of the children and Rosie O'Grady had been tracking Uncle Weatherwise's path for decades. They and I harbored a mutual hatred of Will Wager. We all wanted revenge. The bastard had been responsible for the explosion that killed the kids' parents. And, by labeling my parents as evil incarnate, the weatherman had gotten away with murder."

Hate. Revenge. Strong motives. Could Sophie be the killer?

Sophie smiled, a rueful, small one, but a smile. "If one of them hadn't—*finally*—murdered him, I think I might have."

"Yet, you told Detective Parker about the summer of 1950. You wanted him to know about Kirk Island. If you believe Uncle Weatherwise got what he deserved, why did you want Parker to arrest his killer?"

"Don't you see, Kate? I'm next. I'm only alive because I'm S. J. Corbin. Either Bob or Lucy, who both lost their parents, or Rosie, who lost her lover, want Sophie Provakov dead, too. Revenge for what my parents did."

"I wasn't aware of Lucy's connection to the island," Kate said. She wasn't surprised. "Are the survivors aware of each other? It's strange how they all wound up living in Ocean Vista."

"Maybe, but I don't think so. Rosie had been an adult, only coming to the island on weekends. The two children wouldn't have known her. Lucy's maiden name was Gordon. She's a few years younger than Bob. They probably hadn't known each other either."

"One of them might have figured it out." Kate wondered if that would make a difference. "The killer must have convinced Weatherwise to move here."

Sophie frowning, nodded. "I've followed their lives for years. Lucy's parents died an agonizing death. She found them burned to a crisp. Once she tracked down Weatherwise in Miami, she tried to prosecute him. Even pretended to be his lover. She'd have framed him. Or perjured herself. Or whatever it took to get the bastard behind bars, but she was thwarted at every turn. If Lucy's the killer, she had good reason."

Weird. Her old friend sounded like the defense attorney for a murder suspect who might be planning to make Sophie her next victim.

"Bob Seeley watched his parents die in Kirk Island's tiny hospital. He'd been badly burned, himself. His groin area." Sophie gulped. "For God's sake, Kate, he was only twelve years old. And damaged for life. Bob, too, had started working on his revenge a long time ago, outsmarting both the weatherman and the SEC. I understand most of Weatherwise's millions are now in Bob's Swiss bank account."

Kate nodded. "I know."

"You always were a smart girl. Just watch out. You may be on the killer's hit list." Sophie chewed her lower lip. "Bob's capable of murder. And he was an Army Ranger."

"What about Rosie?"

"I like Rosie, but she's our least likely suspect."

Kate felt foolishly pleased that Sophie had said "our."

"Sure, she'd romanced Albert Anastasia and swears Weatherwise had a part in his hit. But even though my father met Walt Wager in the Park Sheraton's barbershop in 1950, why would that implicate the weatherman in a mob hit all those years later?"

Kate shook her head.

Sophie smiled. "I think Rosie just enjoys spreading rumors about Weatherwise. Causing trouble, casting doubt, trying to destroy his avuncular image any way she could. It's true she lost a boyfriend on Kirk Island, but Rosie's had hundreds of boyfriends. Both before and after the disaster. Would revenging one boyfriend's death be a strong enough motive for two murders?"

A loud knock preempted Kate's response. Maybe Marlene had surfaced. Kate, who'd been distracted by motives, now wondered where her sister-in-law had been all afternoon. She ran through the foyer and opened the door.

Rosie O'Grady, dressed in purple sweats, and carrying an ice bucket holding a bottle of Moët, barged in. "Let's toast the hurricane, Kate. Igor could be our Katrina. The rain's rolling in under my balcony door. And my favorite beach chair just sailed over the railing and out to sea." A blast of thunder accompanied her words.

"Have you seen Marlene?" Kate asked.

"Listen to this," Rosie said. "I just heard that Walt Weatherwise will have one of them serenity panels, a perpetual video with a shatterproof screen, implanted in his tombstone. While the sun shines, it'll run for four hours nonstop, showing clips from his TV forecasts."

Sophie laughed. "How predicable."

"Oh, hi, S.J.," Rosie said. "I didn't see you lurking in the living room."

"Rosie, have you seen Marlene?" Kate raised her voice.

"Yeah. Well, about a half hour ago. I seen her going into Bob Seeley's apartment. Now how about getting us some glasses for the champagne?"

Thirty·eight

"Call Bob Seeley. Ask to speak to Marlene," Kate shouted to Sophie, then dashed out the door.

She reached the elevator, puffing hard, pressed the button, then tried to subdue her panic, taking deep breaths as she waited for it to arrive.

After what seemed like an eternity, she stepped in, willing the damn door to close. She pressed seven, suddenly remembering a long-ago elevator ride with her mother in Bloomingdale's. Her thirteenth birthday. The day she'd shopped for her first bra. The day she'd had her first fight with Marlene.

What the hell was Marlene doing in Bob's apartment? If he'd hurt her, Kate would kill him. For a second she believed she could. Was everyone capable of murder? Weren't human beings made in the likeness of God? Could "the devil made me do it" be a real defense? An explanation for millennia of man's inhumanity to man.

The elevator jerked to a stop. She ran down the corridor and banged on Bob's door.

"Coming. Stop that racket." She heard him before he jerked the door open.

"Where's Marlene?"

"How should I know? First S. J. Corbin questioning me on the phone, now you." He sounded weary. Almost too tired to be angry. His color ashen, his shoulders slumped.

"Rosie saw Marlene go into your apartment."

"Well, she came and went. What's the matter with you, Kate?"

"I don't believe you."

He tried to shut the door, but she pushed past him, yelling, "Marlene!"

"Have you gone mad, woman?" Bob staggered, then came up behind her, and grabbed her left wrist. "Marlene dropped off some condo files for me to take when we evacuate, then left. Do you think I have her chained to the bedpost?"

Kate, whose scenario had been playing out exactly along those lines, hesitated.

"Get out!" Bob put both hands on her shoulders and shoved her through the open door.

Out of the corner of her eye she saw Sophie running down the corridor. "Kate, it's okay. Marlene just called. She was in the office gathering all the important documents and packing them in waterproof briefcases. Said your son, Peter, told her to do that."

Kate's heart fell back in place. With terror evaporating, annoyance took its place. "You'd think she might have let me know."

"Here's something else you should know. Igor is now

officially a Category Five and he's headed straight for Palmetto Beach."

By ten minutes after five, Kate had packed her bags, including Ballou's food, the papers that Jennifer had insisted she bring, and the baby doll, Emma. She'd also showered, washed her hair, and dressed in comfortable sweats, soft cotton socks, and sneakers.

She'd be damned if she'd evacuate without making a Thermos of hot tea, putting on some lipstick and blush, and walking the Westie. She speed-dialed Marlene.

"Believe it or not, Kate, I'm ready to rock and roll."

"Okay. Good. Now, I need a favor. I have to take Ballou for a walk. Please get down to the lobby before five-thirty. Make sure Mary Frances—and the two dolls that I told her she could bring—are on the first bus out." She saw no need to mention to Marlene that Kate herself would be toting Emma.

"Listen, I have to drag that misanthrope next door to you down to the lobby. I want her on the first bus before she changes her mind again and decides to go down with the condo."

"You listen. Mary Frances doesn't want to leave, either. You need to see that she does. If necessary, ride along with her and my crazy neighbor. "I'll try to be down by six. If Ballou and I have to take a later bus, that's fine."

"But Rosie just called. They're already lined up three deep, clamoring to be on the first bus."

"You're the condo president. Pull rank. Just get Mary Frances on board."

"Okay. Okay. Hurry up, Kate."

"See you soon. That's a promise."

Thirty·nine

She heard the wind howl as she stepped out into the pool area. A reluctant Ballou, his ears drooping, followed her. Driving rain pelted her face and the Westie's back; he'd hidden his face under her slicker.

"I don't like this weather any better than you do, Ballou. But we can't have a puddle on the bus, so let's get going." She tugged on his leash. He looked and behaved like an abused and neglected little dog whose cruel mistress wouldn't bring him home.

They crossed to the sand, then turned north toward the pier. The beach was deserted and the dark gray ocean's whitecaps appeared to be a mile high.

Frightened by the thunder, the Westie clung to her side, matching her pace, somehow managing to keep his head covered. A bolt of lightening, on the heels of yet another blast of thunder, made them both jump.

"Hurry up, Ballou." Kate, completely soaked despite

the slicker, wondered how the gathering storm, heralded by such wild weather, could be coming ashore in this ninety-degree heat.

To her delight, Ballou did his business, and they headed home.

"Kate!" A deep voice shouted into the wind. "Over here."

She turned toward the sound. Lucy Diamond, her wet hair plastered to her head, stood on her first-floor balcony, less than a foot above the sand. "I have to talk to you."

"Now?" Kate heard a bus pull into the parking lot. "They're about to start the evacuation."

"Just for a minute." A crash of thunder drowned out Lucy's next few words. Then Kate heard her say, "S. J. Corbin's here. It's about Kirk Island."

Lucy ran inside, closing the balcony door behind her. Damn. "Come on Ballou, we're taking a detour."

The first left off the condo's rear hallway led to Lucy's corridor. Her unit was next to Marlene's. As Kate turned into the empty corridor, she could hear the turmoil in the lobby as the exodus began. If she'd still been in the hallway, she'd have run into the vanguard of evacuees scurrying to the back door.

Lucy was all smiles as she greeted Kate. "Come in, please." She handed Kate a towel. "For Ballou."

Kate thought Lucy, still drenched from standing on her balcony, could use a towel, too.

"Let me take your slicker."

"I won't be here long." Kate dried the Westie, wiping off the damp sand stuck to his paws. Unlike so many of Ocean Vista's residents, Lucy had decorated in primary colors. The striped sofa resembled the U.S. flag. "Where's S.J.?" She'd almost slipped and said "Sophie."

"In the bathroom. Please sit for a moment." Though the words were polite, Lucy's voice had a hard edge.

Kate handed over her slicker, then she and Ballou followed Lucy into the immaculate living room.

Black-and-white framed photographs, mostly beach scenes from the forties, filled every inch of space on all of the tables and the piano. A model sailboat stood on the coffee table next to one of the larger photographs. Kate, squinting at the hull, read the sloop's name: LUCY KAT. And her home port: KIRK ISLAND.

The wind whipped against the balcony door and Lucy wept, wailing louder than the wind.

Startled, Kate looked up.

"My parents died from radiation poisoning, but you knew that, didn't you, Kate?" She'd stopped crying, and her strident voice had become childlike, but there was a gun in her right hand.

Kate felt torn between pity and terror.

"You and S. J. Corbin, aka Sophie Provakov, underestimated me, Kate. I'm a former federal prosecutor. I bugged your apartment." She gestured to the right. "Walk down the hall. You can wait out the hurricane evacuation with your old friend and fellow traitor."

Ballou stayed at Kate's side, watching Lucy, seeming to focus on the gun, which Lucy had just switched to her left hand. With her right hand, Lucy used a key to open the door to the guest bathroom. "Get in there." She poked Kate with barrel of the gun.

Sophie lay on the tile floor, bleeding from a gash in her forehead.

Lucy pulled the door shut and Kate heard the key turn in the lock.

Kate grabbed a couple towels, placing one under Sophie's head, and holding the other against her forehead. Sophie didn't move, but she was breathing.

Double damn. Kate's cell phone was packed away in her tote bag, along with all those important papers that no longer mattered. Marlene had probably left on the first bus, believing Kate would be right behind her. But Kate was locked in Lucy's bathroom with shocking pink flamingos cavorting on the wallpaper.

Sophie stirred.

"That's a good boy, Ballou." Kate petted the Westie, who nuzzled against her, then sat near the shower.

Kate stuck a pink plastic glass under the cold water, then held it to Sophie's lips. The head wound was still bleeding. Kate rummaged around in the medicine cabinet and found a bottle of peroxide and a box of Band-Aids.

She knelt next to her patient, applying the peroxide with the corner of a clean towel. "This may smart a bit."

Sophie groaned, then yelled, "Stop."

"Hold still, Humpty Dumpty, I want to tape you back together."

"Very funny," Sophie said, but she stopped squirming.

"Okay. That should control the bleeding." Kate stood up.

"Can I sit up?"

"If you're not too dizzy," Kate spoke with more assurance than she felt. It had been decades since she played nurse. "What happened?"

"I objected to being locked in the bathroom. Lucy used the butt of her gun to convince me."

"No windows in the guest bathroom." Kate wanted to cry. "No way to escape."

"I guess we'll ride out the hurricane here."

Kate sank to the floor, sitting next to Sophie. By the time Marlene realized that they hadn't made it to the shelter, it would probably be too late for anyone to come back to ground zero.

Forty

The room rocked her awake. Good God, the building was swaying!

How long had she been dozing? Ballou, tucked in her arm, licked her hand, comforting Kate, but not making any noise. Sophie slept, her head propped up on three bath towels. Two beach towels covered her shoulders and chest. Lucy had a well-stocked linen closet.

It had been the longest night of Kate's life. Watching the clock, finally accepting that the last bus must have left Ocean Vista. Wondering if Lucy would reappear. Wishing Sophie wasn't in so much pain. Waiting for the hurricane to hit.

Even in this windowless prison, she could hear the howling wind and torrential rain. Pounding. Crashing. Like standing on the tarmac next to a 747 ready for take-off. She glanced at her watch. Ten minutes to seven. Igor had arrived ahead of schedule.

The bathroom listed to the left. Bottles of shampoo and body lotion flew off the shelf next to the sink. Water seeped in under the door. Oh God, they were going to drown in here.

Sophie woke up screaming.

The lights on either side of the mirror went off, leaving them in the dark.

Something heavy slammed against the outside of the building. Maybe Ocean Vista would collapse and they'd be crushed to death. Which would be the easier way to die?

Ballou barked, scratching at the door.

Kate banged on the door, shouted, "Lucy, let us out!" To her surprise, the lock turned, and Lucy opened the door.

"Come with me." A very wet Lucy pointed the gun at Ballou's head.

Kate helped Sophie up. "Can you walk?"

Staggering, Sophie nodded.

The water in the dark hall came up to Kate's shins.

"Get in front of me, go into the living room. I'll shoot the dog if you don't do what I say." Lucy slurred *say*—it sounded like "chay."

Great. Crazy and drunk.

As they entered the living room, a huge wave crashed through the wide open space where the balcony door used to be.

"It's your turn to die, Sophie," Lucy cried.

Ballou darted from Kate's side and bit Lucy's leg, drawing blood. She aimed the gun at Ballou and, as a screaming Kate ran toward the Westie, pulled the trigger, but missed the moving target.

The ocean rolled in, waves flooded the living room, knocking Lucy to her knees.

Kate watched in horror as Lucy was swept away, her body flying out onto the water-covered beach.

She grabbed Ballou and yelled to Sophie. "Run to the front door. As soon as we get out, slam it shut."

They dashed through the corridor, the ocean on their heels. Kate yanked open the steel door to the stairwell, dragged Sophie in, and closed the door behind them.

"We have to get to the top floor."

"I can't, Kate."

"You can and you will. Ocean Vista was built in the sixties. This stairwell is solid cement. If we can climb up high enough, we'll survive."

Panting, they fumbled their way up seven fights of stairs.

Channel Eight's new weatherman was aboard the helicopter that rescued them from the roof that evening.

Epilogue

Three Days Later

The sun sparkling on the now calm Atlantic reminded Kate why they'd migrated to South Florida. As Herb served a second round of drinks on the Neptune Inn's deck, she felt relaxed, almost festive.

Mary Frances raised her wine glass. "To surviving Hurricane Igor."

"I'll drink to that." Marlene held up her martini. "But with considerably less enthusiasm."

Most of the damage to Ocean Vista had been minimal, but Marlene's condo, right next to Lucy's, had been totally trashed by the storm. She'd moved in with Kate.

"We'll go shopping," Kate said, trying to sound positive. Marlene had lost all her treasures, along with all her clutter. "As soon as the contractors finish up, we'll have fun redecorating."

"I guess," Marlene said. "I'm just glad I brought all three of my wedding albums with me."

"Thank God, my dolls were spared." Mary Frances looked up toward heaven.

Kate nudged Marlene's knee, nonverbally begging her not to comment.

"You gotta get a life, Mary Frances," Rosie said. "Then you gotta get a guy in your life. I tell you what. You teach the tango in my dance class and I'll find you a boyfriend."

The former nun blushed, but nodded.

Not wanting to talk about romance, Kate changed the subject. "Can you believe Bob never came back from the shelter?"

"I wonder how he'll like living in Switzerland?" Marlene laughed. "The winters will be a lot colder."

"He'll have his millions to keep him warm." Rosie turned to Kate. "Where's S. J. Corbin? Ain't she coming back to Ocean Vista? Weatherwise's apartment is high and dry. She could move in."

Another subject Kate didn't want to address. "S.J.'s retiring. She left the hospital yesterday, packed a few things, and flew to California to check out Carmel." Sophie had told Kate her quest was over. That she needed to make a new start. And finally put the past behind her. She'd advised Kate to do the same, then kissed her good-bye.

"What did Nick Carbone say, Kate?" Mary Frances asked. "Did he read you the riot act for playing Miss Marple . . . *again*?"

Kate sighed. "Yes. And no. He called and gave me hell, then asked me out to dinner."